For Wayne van der Stelt
and Alan Sultan,

And for my family

This project has been assisted by
the Commonwealth Government
through the Australia Council, its
arts funding and advisory body.

A Vintage Book
published by
Random House Australia Pty Ltd
20 Alfred Street, Milsons Point, NSW 2061
http://www.randomhouse.com.au

Sydney   New York   Toronto
London   Auckland   Johannesburg
and agencies throughout the world

First published 1995
This edition published 1998

National Library of Australia
Cataloguing-in-Publication Data

Tsiolkas, Christos.
    Loaded.

    ISBN 0 09 183941 6.

    I. Title.
    A823.3

Cover design by Yolande Gray
Typeset by Midland Typesetters, Maryborough
Printed by Griffin Paperbacks, Adelaide

10 9 8 7 6 5 4

Christos Tsiolkas was born in Melbourne in 1965. He grew up in a bilingual household where he learnt politics and music as well as how to make a pretty good Turkish coffee. *Loaded*, his first novel, was published in 1995. In 1996 he collaborated with Sasha Soldatow on the dialogue, *Jump Cuts*, also published by Random House. He has written fiction, essays, criticism and reviews for a range of publications (commercial and lo-fi) as well as working with super-8 film, video and graphics. In 1998 he co-wrote the collaborative theatre piece, *Who's Afraid of the Working Class?* for Melbourne Workers Theatre. Christos is a Scorpio astrologically, an anarchist or socialist politically (depending on who's in power) and a film freak socially. He is currently living in Canberra with his lover, Wayne van der Stelt and is a supporter of the Richmond and Ainslie football clubs. His second novel, *The Jesus Man*, will be published in 1999. Christos Tsiolkas believes John Howard has been put on earth by hostile aliens.

The immigrant child has the advantage or the burden of knowing what other children may more easily forget: a child, any child, necessarily lives in his own time, his own room. The child cannot have a life identical with that of his mother or father. For the immigrant child this knowledge is inescapable.

Richard Rodriguez *An American writer*

EAST

Sister Sledge *Lost in music*

The morning is ending

The morning is ending and I've just opened my eyes. I stare across the cluttered room I'm in. I yawn. I scratch at my groin. I feel my cock and start a slow masturbation. When I'm finished, and it doesn't take long, I get up with a leap, wrap a towel around my naked body and make a slow journey downstairs.

I hear noises from throughout the house. A robotic voice is squealing over a bass-beat on the CD. The very narrow stairs stretch down before me. I walk past cobwebs, stains on the carpet, a biro on one step, a cigarette butt on another. In the lounge I grab a packet of cigarettes and light one. On the mantelpiece I notice an old family photo. I've forgotten this photo. My brother in a red shirt and black shorts has one arm around the old man and another around my mum. She looks like Elizabeth Taylor, or at least is trying to, and Dad is wearing a grey suit with a narrow black tie. He's trying to look like Mastroianni, or like Delon. The tie belongs to me now. I'm in the picture too. Sitting cross-legged on the grass, in a blue shirt, aiming a plastic gun at the camera. The colours in the photo are rich, bright. Colour photos don't do that any more. Technology makes things look too real. I turn away from the photograph and look at last night's mess strewn across the lounge room. It's not my place.

In the kitchen Peter is cooking bacon and eggs. Janet is sitting reading him something from the paper. George, one of the boys they live with, is sitting across from her. He smiles up at me and I return him a cool smile, nothing too eager. He's in pyjama bottoms and through the slit I catch a glimpse of pubic hair. All I want to do is touch him but I look away. Janet stops reading.

–Want some food? I nod, take a seat, try not to look at

George. My head hurts and I wish I was home. Peter slips me a smile and asks me if I have a hangover. I nod and Janet laughs at me.

–Poor baby, she smirks. Corrupted by his brother's friends. Her voice rings loud in my head. This morning she is a study in red. Her hair dyed burgundy, a red floral dress over her fleshy pale body, pink slippers on her feet. She's reading the sports pages of the newspaper and I grab a glimpse of the front–page headlines. Australia have won the First Test. I've just got up and I'm already bored. I wouldn't mind a joint.

–Have you got any gear left? I ask my brother.

–Breakfast and coffee first. Then you have to ring Mum and then you can roll your own joint.

–You can make your own coffee too, blurts out Janet. Peter gives her half a dirty look. I catch it and feel immediately better. I'm his little brother. He's got to look after me. I eat the food quickly and gulp down some water. George is laughing at me. He slowly picks at the food on his plate. I try to say something to him but my mouth is too full of egg. He leans over and wipes some food from my bottom lip. He smells of fresh sweat, dry come and tobacco. My cock goes hard and I don't try to speak, just scoff down the food.

Someone has changed the music upstairs and disco comes wafting into the kitchen.

–Turn it up, yells George, and the volume increases. I tap the edge of the table in time with the music. Peter puts on a pot of coffee then comes over to me and grabs me from behind. He sways from side to side, crooning the song into my ear. I giggle and tell him to fuck off.

–You fuck off, Ari, he laughs. Go have a shower and stop parading your young flesh around us old–timers. I give him a brotherly kiss.

In the bathroom I put the radio on and a slow sensual wail

comes out. A middle-eastern chant above a techno drum pattern. I inspect my face in the mirror and scrub away a faint trace of egg and dry spit around my mouth. I turn the water on full blast and sing along to the radio. Wiping away the smells of sweat, alcohol, dope, I sing along to the radio, louder and louder. My mouth is still dry, even with all this water and I put some toothpaste in my mouth and gargle. When I'm finished I stand in front of the mirror, wiping myself dry, wiping myself clean. The throbbing in my head has gone and I start reading a postcard on the mirror. Women's liberation stuff. An old woman with a banner that reads: We hold up half the sky. She looks very tired. Lots of lines on her face like someone who must have smoked too much.

  –Coffee, I demand, coming back into the kitchen. Janet is about to say something rude to me but I rush to her and kiss her hard on the cheek. Thanks for the coffee, sis, I say to her, and rush out and up the stairs. I'm not your sister, I hear her scream, I'm only sleeping with your brother, I'm not married to him. But I don't give a shit. My voice gets louder and louder climbing the stairs, grabbing at the cobwebs, singing along to whatever music is playing in the house. I put on my tracksuit pants and my T-shirt and rush down the stairs again.

  –Coffee, I scream again, and Janet flicks a grape into my face. I catch it in my mouth, roll it out on my tongue and spit it back to her. She turns her face away but George grabs the grape in mid-air and puts it in his mouth. That was my spit, I whisper. I whisper down deep inside me so no one can hear.

  –Call Mum. Peter holds the phone out to me. I get up and start dialling. Janet asks Peter why I've got an image of Africa on my T-shirt. Mum, I say, how are you, I slept over at Panayioti's house. He's anti-racist I hear Peter say, not adding that it's an old T-shirt of his. Yeah, I'll come home soon, I tell Mum. No, I don't think he's coming up. Are you coming home? I ask Peter. I am home, he says. He's not coming up, Mum. I don't know, maybe he's busy. She asks me if Janet is there. I start talking in Greek, trying to be discreet. She wants to talk to Peter or Janet. I say goodbye and hand the phone to my brother. I'm all for racism, I tell Janet, moving slowly towards her, rolling my eyes and putting on a mean motherfucker sneer, dropping my voice very low. I think every whitey deserves to get it in the throat, I whisper in her ear. How about you? she counters, moving away. You're white. I just look at her. I'm not white, I'm a wog. You're white, she insists. I say nothing because the conversation is boring. I'm just talking crap to get at her. I read the papers, I see the news, I talk to people; white, black, yellow, pink, they're all fucked. The T-shirt feels heavy on me. Wrong T-shirt to bring to this house.

    –You're European, aren't you? George asks me. So you're white as well. Maybe, I answer, and don't say anything else. I don't want to start an argument with any of them. It will go on forever. The T-shirt I'm wearing feels heavy on me.

    –Can I have a joint? I ask.

Only if you answer me, says George. A sudden fury consumes me. I clam up and look at my coffee. It's dark and strong smelling. I ask again. Can I have a joint? He smiles at me, shakes his head, gets up and goes into the lounge room. When he comes in he sits down close to me and rolls a joint. I look at him. He hasn't shaved or washed and a coat of thin hair is growing on his chest. He lights the joint and blows the first wave of smoke into my face. I breathe it in and grin at him, then look over to my brother, who's arguing on the phone. George passes the joint to me.

I take three strong drags before passing it over to Janet. She takes a small puff and then passes it to Peter. He smokes like me. Long, strong drags. I look down into my coffee. Anything not to look at George. The smoke is making me high and the kitchen seems bigger than before, full of unfamiliar objects. My eyes wander around the posters. I

notice the colours of the Aboriginal flag behind Janet. I look
at small pictures of movie stars and pop stars. Ronald Reagan
in a bikini. A poster advertising *Gimme Shelter* which Peter
had in his room at home. That and a portrait of Debbie
Harry were the only posters he took from our house. He
left the soccer prints behind. My mind is drifting. I reach
for one of George's cigarettes and light it. The nicotine
straightens me out a little. I hear Janet and Peter having an
argument. The joint is back to me.

–What's Mum want? I ask.

–Your ass, kiddo. My brother comes up to me and slaps
me lightly on the back of the head. She wants you home
for lunch. Us as well, adds Janet, looking sour. I look up at
the clock. It's nearly twelve. I'm not going home for lunch,
I say, so you two don't have to either. Is she calling back?
Peter nods.

George shakes his head. She always rings, he says. Janet
nods her head in agreement and Peter looks embarrassed.
I just shrug my shoulders. You're lucky she rings, I think to
myself, it means you don't have to waste money ringing her.
Janet passes me a cigarette. For a moment I'm in her good
books because I got her out of going to lunch. She lights
my cigarette for me. Ta, I say. The phone rings and I jump
up to get it.

–A barrage of Greek hits me and I suddenly realise I'm
stoned. Hi, Mum. I take a deep puff of the cigarette and
listen. When she's finished I say slowly, making sure I'm not
slurring my words, Mum, I'll see you in the afternoon.
Another burst of yelling in Greek. They're not coming, I tell
her, they're both studying this afternoon. Bullshit, she says
loudly in English. She tells me to come straight home, I tell
her I'll come when I want to and we hang up on each other.

–You're all studying if she asks, I say, and I go over to the
sink to get some more water. My mouth is dry from the
smoke and I'm hungry. A stoned hunger that's like a deep
cavern inside me, nothing to do with my head or my heart,

a cavern in the stomach that I need to fill. I put some toast on. George gets up and heads off towards the shower. I start rolling another joint. The morning is slipping into afternoon and the sun has seeped into the kitchen. All the colours in the room are dancing in the sunlight.

-Can I take this with me? I ask, holding up the joint. Peter nods and Janet takes up the paper again. I eat my toast, not bothering to butter it, and then get up.

Upstairs in the spare room I pack up my stuff in my sports bag, take out my Walkman and hook the earphones around my neck. Music is still coming from a room down the hall. And the smell of dope. I don't recognise the song. I'm careful walking down the narrow staircase and go kiss my brother goodbye. He smells of milk and soap. I kiss Janet's cheek and she tugs at my hair. She smells of soap too. She smells like Peter. Thanks for letting me crash, I say. I bang on the bathroom door. George pokes his head out of the door, a towel over his shoulder. His upper arms are hairless, tanned, flabby. I nod at him and leave the house.

The day is warm and the sun stabs hard at my eyes. I put the headphones on my ears, blink and turn the Walkman on.

Riding on a bus

Riding on a bus always makes me horny, something to do with the sensation of moving while looking down into the world below. I sink behind a seat in the back and shift my tight cock. The music enters my head and I rock back and forth a little to a pulsating, electric beat.

I get off the bus in the city and walk across Russell Street to one of the video arcades. The Chinese boys and girls are checking each other out, dressed up for the Saturday afternoon. Inside the arcade solitary boys are gazing fixedly into video screens and groups are clustered around the

bigger machines. I see my Greek friend Joe and stop the
Walkman. Rhythm is replaced by a cacophony of electronic
whistles. He nods at me and looks back at the screen. I
stand beside the terminal and gaze around the room. Video
arcades give me a headache. A balding guy with a beer gut
is standing at the counter exchanging notes for coins. His
belly button is peering out of his shirt, his remaining hair is
greasy and thin. Ugly. He notices my stare and focuses on
me. I keep my eye on him for a second then turn back to
the screen.

Joe gets done by the video opponent and smashes his
hand hard onto the side of the terminal. Let's grab a coffee,
he says. I follow him round the corner to Lonsdale Street,
swinging my bag behind me. He's got himself a new crew
cut and is wearing a dirty black T-shirt. The nice Chinese
and Greek couples step out of his way. The men in clean
ironed shirts, buttoned up to the collar if they are Asian,
unbuttoned to the chest if they are wog. The girls, Asian or
wog, are in red and black, all wearing short skirts. I nod to
some of the women, seeking some acknowledgment, testing
my looks. I don't bother checking out the boys; no use
cruising when girls are around. Joe sits at a table outside a
Greek coffee shop, lies back in the chair, closes his eyes
and takes in the sun. I sit in the shade. It's getting hot. At
another table is a middle-aged man talking non-stop to a
young woman. She's got on too much lipstick, too much
perfume. She's got a bad woggy haircut; too much hairspray
makes her hair look like a wig.

–Got a job yet? Joe asks me. I hate that question. No, I
answer and put the Walkman in my bag. He starts telling
me about his job. Working people always think you'll be
interested in what they do. None that I know do anything
interesting.

–Looking for work? I say yes and get up to ask for coffee.
Joe calls out for a milkshake and takes a five-dollar bill from
his pocket. My shout, I say. Make it mine; he disagrees,

you're unemployed. The young woman looks up at me. I don't take the money and go into the shop. The cavern in my stomach is still there, in my blood, my whole system calling for food. I order a cake with the drinks.

-How's your folks? Joe asks me. The longer we are friends the less interesting are the questions we ask each other. I give him the usual answers and grab a cigarette from a squashed packet in my bag. How's yours?

-Good.

-Going home to watch the cricket? I don't answer. He knows I hate the game. We going out tonight? I ask.

-Sure. Meet you at my place. I nod and eat the cake quickly. Syrup coats my mouth and I grab a napkin to clean myself up. The dope is wearing off and Joe is busy checking out the girls around him. Some nice birds here, he whispers with a grin. I give them a quick glance. Too woggy, I say. There is one woman I find attractive; a young girl in a black sweater, her hair in a ponytail, a line of soft red lipstick on her lips. I like that one, I say to Joe, and she notices me pointing. I smile at her and she smiles back.

-You're in man, she'll give you a root. Joe is an idiot when it comes to sex. Talks like a cheap Italian movie.

-I don't root, I fuck, I tell him.

-What's the diff? I shrug my shoulders and butt out my cigarette. The way you do it, I say and stand up.

-The guy she's with is one ugly fuck, isn't he? I look at the guy. He's young, wearing a bad floral shirt. Joe's wrong. He's got a good body, a mildly handsome face. It's his clothes that are the problem. I don't saying anything to Joe, he gets uncomfortable when I talk about boys.

-I've got a joint in my pocket, I tell him patting my tracksuit pocket. Want some? He agrees.

We go to smoke in Joe's car in the underground car park. The young security person looks stoned and waves hello to us. He's sitting with his legs up on the counter, reading the paper. The cricket is on the radio and Joe starts a conversation. I walk off and search for his car. There is a cool breeze in the car park and when I find the car I rest against it and put my bag on its roof. His parents bought it for him for his eighteenth birthday, and over the two years he has washed it religiously every Sunday; he even vacuums the back seat. I don't drive. I don't need to. Everyone I know has a car.

-Take your fucking bag off my car. Joe comes over and searches the roof for any scratches. He glares at me as I get into the passenger seat. I take out the joint and offer him the first smoke. He takes it and lets out a long slow exhale of smoke.

Joe has got his world worked out, or so he likes to think he has. He's got a job, got a girlfriend, got a car. Soon he wants to get married. I think it's a mistake but I figure that it isn't my business to tell him such things and I don't. He's an adult. But it seems to me that there are two things in this world guaranteed to make you old and flabby. Work and marriage. It is inevitable. The faces of all the workers and all the married people I see carry the strain of living a life of rules and regulations. Joe's face is still young looking, he still has sharp bright eyes. But he's changing. Doing the nine to five on weekdays. No dirty T-shirts but a shirt and tie and a briefcase by his side. He keeps his crew cut because he still wants to dip one foot into the pool of freedom, but even that will change once the wedding ring is slipped on. They won't let him walk up the aisle without at least two inches of hair, not in a Greek church. It's his cop-out.

Unless you're a smart thief everyone has to work, or scrounge around saying yes-sir-no-sir-can-I-have-a-raise-sir-can-I-have-the-day-off-sir-my-grandmother-is-sick-sir-dad-can-you-lend-me-twenty. We all have to sell ourselves. But you don't have to get married, you don't have to sell all of yourself. There is a small part of myself, deep inside of me, which I let no one touch. If I let it out, let someone have a look at it, brush their hands across that part of my soul, then they would want to have it, buy it, steal it, own it. Joe's put that part of himself up for market and he would be the first to say it's because he can't put up with the demands. Parents, friends, bosses, girlfriends, girlfriends' parents, cousins, aunts, uncles, even the fucking neighbours. They all want to sell, buy, invest in the future. And now he's just waiting for the right bid, and I know what it is. Once his parents and her parents offer a house, or at least a hefty deposit, the deal will be clinched. The marriage will be arranged. Joe will have joined the other side, just another respectable wog on a mortgage. I look at him drawing on the joint and I turn away and make circles in the air with the smoke. Coward, I whisper. But he doesn't hear me.

–What you say? Nothing, I reply and he gives me the joint. We smoke it and he offers me a lift home but I prefer to walk. It is a good half-hour but I want to clear my head from the alcohol last night. I get out and confirm meeting at his place tonight. Joe waves me away and goes off to have a conversation with the security guard. I shuffle around my bag and find my Walkman.

Dad is in the garden

Dad is in the garden watering the plants. The garden is the most important part of his life now. If he's not among the plants, he's asleep, or down at the coffee shop with his friends. That's when he's not working, but I don't know what Dad is like at work. We don't talk about it.

I go up to him and gently touch his shoulder. He pulls away. Go see your mother, he says, she's upset. He yanks the Walkman out of my hand. Where have you been you animal?

–With Panayioti. He walks away and fiddles with some flowers. I hear him muttering about me, about my brother, about my sister. I expected his anger, I'm used to it, but at the same time the whole of my emotions, all the shit fluttering around my head, feels like it's going to erupt out of me and all over him. My body is immediately tense, waiting for the fight. I yell arsehole at him. He hears and shakes his head. Then he looks sad and I wish I could walk straight past the gate, back down the street and away from him, my family and the world. But I don't. I walk in the front door.

Mum's smoking a cigarette in the kitchen and listening to the radio. I smell tomato and eggs and hope the shouting is over quickly. I'm starving. She begins and I shut off. It's an easy trick I have learned. I focus on her forehead. Peter taught me the trick but we use it to different results. Dad can rave at him for hours and Peter will walk away unaffected. It's Mum who drives him crazy. But I have no patience for my mother. Dad has an excuse, he was born in Greece. A different world. Poverty, war, hardship, no school, no going out, no TV. It's a world he'd prefer to go back to and a world I have no fucking clue about. Singing around coffee tables, sleeping in the afternoon, walks in the evening and celebrations in the night. He should never have left, no matter how bad things were back there. Here, under the Australian sun, he's constantly sniffing the air and looking disappointed. He can't really breathe here, he says.

But Mum's different. She was born here and is as Australian as me. Shit, with the nasally squawk she speaks in she's more skip than me. She butts out her cigarette and lets fly. Where have I been? Why don't I ring? I stare into her forehead. The questions continue and I don't answer any of them. She starts a rave in Greek, calls me a fucking animal, a pig in the mud she stresses, throws a tea-towel at me and starts crying. I go to her, put my arm around her shoulder and kiss her on the cheek. Hi Mum, I say, I'm hungry. She slaps me lightly on my arse and, grumbling a little more, starts preparing lunch.

I turn on the TV in the lounge room and flick across the stations. A young James Stewart in a cowboy suit. I sit down to watch the movie and Mum brings in a plate of tomato and egg, some fetta, some bread and a salad. Do you want some meatballs? she asks me, and I refuse. Some coke? I nod and she brings me a full glass and sets it down on the table.

–I used to fight with your grandfather all the time, Ari. I scoop the meal in my mouth, wrapping the fetta in bread and swallowing it in large bites. But I always respected him, Ari. Always. She says the last words in Greek.

–I respect you too, Mum. And Dad too. It's a lie and maybe she knows it. I love my parents but I don't think they have much guts. Always complaining about how hard life is and not having much money. And they do shit to change any of it. Dad would like to go back to Greece some day, he thinks that life will change for him then. But Mum wouldn't leave us behind and I don't know if Greece would make her any happier. I don't know what would make her happier; she must dream of blinking her eyes, finding herself sixteen again and making different decisions.

–I'm sorry Mum. I got drunk and forgot to ring. And I didn't get up till late.

–Just like your brother to get you drunk. She looks at me, smiles a little. Is he at the library? she asks. Yes, I lie, he'll be there all day.

–You can tell me, she says, he's gone out with Janet, hasn't he? I just stare at the TV. He's studying, Mum. I finish off the food and she starts clearing away the mess. I never see your brother any more. Not since that bitch took him away from us, I hear her yell loudly from the kitchen.

On screen an ugly bad guy has started a fight with Jimmy Stewart. A blonde woman in tight black suspenders and a white petticoat helps him out by smashing a bottle of spirits over the bad guy's head. She's got great legs and no talent. You can see her eyes wandering towards the camera. I'm not listening to Mum. She can go on about my brother having left home for ages. She broods, cries about it, holds her head low sometimes, sighing deeply, lamenting her boy's betrayal of her. Yet she nurses the betrayal, cultivates it, makes her pain ecstatic because it adds a sheen of tragedy to a boring life. I let her rave and watch the movie. Soon she gives up on me and weeps silently to herself in the kitchen, doing the dishes.

There must be thousands of movies I've seen on television. It could be that the one I'm watching now I've seen years before. The best run early on weekday mornings and I often go to bed setting the alarm for 2.15 am or 3.35 am. I wake up in the middle of the night, grab some biscuits and chips from the pantry, or a glass of whisky, or roll a joint, whatever addiction I need to satisfy at that moment, and watch an old movie. There are fewer ads at that time of night and there is no one else around making noise, asking questions, ruining the film for you. I don't talk much about movies to people. I prefer to watch them on my own, even at the cinema. Everyone around me talks about loving the movies but that's bullshit. They'll go to see a movie because everyone is talking about it, or they need to do something before dinner or clubbing, or because the ads for the movie are good. Most people prefer television. I hate television, only watch it to catch up with old movies. People on television – actors, journalists, entertainers – are all second-rate. Movies are movies. They're an occasion, a night out. Television is a piece of furniture.

   An ad comes on the television and I jump to my feet. Mum, I yell, where's Alex? At your aunt's, Mum yells back. She comes in with her packet of cigarettes in her hand. I grab two from her and light them both. I hand one back to her. There you go, Bette, I say. She looks at me with a puzzled expression. Mum is part of the television generation as well, and she knows shit about anything except what the television and magazines tell her. Brain dead. For her the real world begins every day at seven in the morning with 'Good Morning Australia'.

-I'm going over. Do you want to come? She shakes her head. I kiss her goodbye, yell something neutral in Greek to my father who ignores me, hitch the Walkman around my track pants and put the headphones on. I press play and walk out the gate.

A Vietnamese woman

A Vietnamese woman, thin and dressed in a white singlet, dark glasses over her eyes, walks towards me on Church Street. I wave to her and take off the headphones. She stops for a chat. Trin is lovely, with dark shimmering skin, but she's smacked out most of the time and never takes the sunglasses off. Our conversation is stilted. I ask after her kid and she becomes a bit more animated, telling me she's left him with her parents for the weekend. She loves her child. She walks with me to the bottom of the hill and I invite her into my aunt's place but she declines. I don't blame her. The Greeks, the Vietnamese, the skips, the whole fucking neighbourhood is suspicious of her. She avoids people as much as possible, except for the junkies and people like me who don't wish her any harm. The rumour is she whores for a living but I've never asked and I don't care a shit either way. She told me once, with her broken accent, in her soft voice made raw by cigarettes, that Ari, you know, it not true what they say about me. Sure, mate, I told her, anyway, a living is a living. It didn't seem to be the answer she wanted but I wasn't going to pretend that I believed her completely. A junkie needs cash. It's not my business to blame her. Nor is it my business to absolve her.

Trin says *ciao* to me outside my aunt's house and walks back up the hill. Take care, I say softly and hope that my whisper wraps around her slight shoulders and comforts her a little.

My aunt's home smells of basil and lemon and I walk straight through to the back. My aunt and my sister Alex are sitting at the kitchen table and my aunt is reading the coffee cups. I kiss them both and get a big hug from my aunt.

–What are the coffee cups saying, *Thea* Tasia? I ask in Greek.

–Shut up, Alex says, we haven't finished mine. I ignore her. Can you read mine as well, *Thea*? She nods and I start making some Greek coffee. While I stir the sugar and coffee in the *briki* I listen to what she's telling Alex. She sees a snake being trodden on by someone. That's a good sign. Some friend of Alex's is talking behind her back but Alex is going to get even with her. She sees a black spot in the home with a 'J' close to it. That part is bullshit. Like my mother, my aunt blames Janet for my brother leaving home. Alex has the good sense to ignore that part. I bring the coffee to the boil and pour some for myself. I get a glass of water from the fridge, sit down next to them and drink the coffee as fast as I can. The mixture of dope and caffeine is rushing through my system, sending the blood into spasms and I'm fidgety. My aunt notices. We'll be with you soon, she says. Alex kicks me under the table. Wait your turn. I finish the coffee and turn the cup upside down to let the sediment dry.

A lot of Greek bullshitters read the coffee cups but I reckon my Aunt Tasia is the real thing. She'll make up stuff, of course. She always foretells wedding rings and jobs; you have to ignore that part of the reading. Alex dips her finger into the bottom of the sediment in her cup and my aunt has a look at it. I see a 'C', yes it's an English 'C', and your heart is encircled by it. Do you know any boy starting with 'C' Aleka? My sister lies. No, *Thea*. I keep a straight face and ask what else she sees. My aunt looks a little concerned.

She makes the sign of the cross but doesn't answer me.

She reads my coffee slowly, turning the cup around and around in her hands. I stare at her face, at her hair; look at the strands of grey hair peeping through the dyed blonde curls. There is someone who is wanting to look after you, Ari, someone who cares for you, but you are not facing them. You are ignoring them. She points to a few blobs of dried coffee. I can make out figures in the blobs. A line does divide the figures. Their name begins with a *gamma*. I know immediately it is George. I can even smell a faint trace of his sweat in the room. I say nothing. I feel foolish about the thought.

Alex gets up and puts a Greek record on the stereo. A slow, old *tsamiko*. My aunt begins to sway a little to the music.

Someone is going to offer you a job, Ari. I see a long road but there is money at the end of it. I smile at her and look to where she is pointing in the coffee cup. I see the road but the blob at the end of it is just a blob. Alex comes over to have a look. What's the job, Thea? she asks. A garbage collector? She laughs and dances away from us. My aunt bangs the table and tells her to shut up.

Continue reading, I tell her, and just ignore the little bitch. I'm not really offended. I'd hate any job she would have mentioned. Alex moves away and continues her solitary *tsamiko* and I press my thumb into the sediment. We both look at it. The perpendicular lines of the *gamma* are clear in the middle of the black muck. I tell you, Ari, she says, a girl whose name begins with a *gamma* is going to steal your heart. I avoid her eyes. I can taste George's sweat. I lean over and kiss her. How are you? I ask.

–Like shit, she answers. Alex tells me you stayed at your brother's last night. Is he alright?

–Yes, he's fine. He sends his love. My aunt makes a face. Sure, sure, she mutters, but he can't find the time to visit his *thea*. I ignore her and ask after my cousins. Sam's at the shop and Katerina is out watching a movie. She asks me if I want something to eat and I refuse. She asks me again, pleading with me, and I refuse again. I get up and say I have to go. Alex is still dancing and I kiss my aunt goodbye, tell Alex I'll see her later at home. On the way out I use the phone to ring Phil's place. I ring once, let it ring through twice. I hang up and ring again, letting it ring twice again. On the third try I let Phil answer the phone. Who is it? he asks. Ari. It's fine, come over. I yell *gia sou* to my sister and aunt and I'm out of the door, Walkman on. The blast of music wipes out the world in front of my eyes.

Two rings for two grams

Two rings for two grams of speed. Phil is a small-time dealer with a bad case of paranoia. Every time he walks out of his house he scans the street for cops and whenever he hears a helicopter up above he looks out the window to make sure it's not hovering over his house. I couldn't live so tense. No drug is worth it. The phone makes him nervous and that's why I have to ring a few times in a row, so he knows it's not a bugged phone call. He's organising getting a beeper so we can communicate in numbered code. It would be a good thing. Relax him a little.

I walk to the cash machine on Bridge Road and take out one hundred and fifty dollars. I buy a packet of cigarettes, not exchanging a word with the woman at the milk bar, just pointing to the fags I want, and still listening to the music on my machine. I spend fifteen minutes in a newsagent flicking through magazines. I read a couple of music magazines and scan the pictures in *Time*. I beat time with my shoe to the music.

The Walkman is my favourite toy. It creates a soundtrack for me and lets me slip into walking through a movie. The tape I've got on at the moment I put together the other week at my cousin's house. A few sad songs, a few fast songs, a few songs I never heard of but I liked the look of the CD covers.

This is an up tape, it makes me walk faster, keeps me at a distance from the people brushing past me. I like music. More than that, I love music but I'm definite in my tastes. Soul. Hard rock and punk. I listen to heaps. Heavy metal is mostly shit though some thrash metal is okay (on speed or after a few bongs). Rap I like. Of course. Some disco, not high-energy, but house. Jazz means nothing to me because I can't understand it. I love Greek music but only the old stuff. I'm definite in my tastes.

On this tape I'm listening to I have the Jackson Five doing 'I want you back'. This is a supreme moment in music history, even if I'm the only one in the world who knows it. On one of my tapes I have one side of the cassette playing only that song. When things aren't going so well I play that cassette over and over and just walk around the city or walk around Richmond. I sit on a rock by the river throwing bread to the ducks, letting a young Michael Jackson cheer me up. In the three minutes it takes the song to play I'm caught in a magic world of harmony and joy, a truly ecstatic joy, where the aching longing to be somewhere else, out of this city, out of this country, out of this body and out of this life, is kept at bay. I relive those three minutes again and again till I'm calm enough to walk back into life again. I can't meditate in silence, I haven't got the patience. I meditate to music; I need something else going on.

The old Greek men are playing cards in the coffee shops. A group of rich kids from the eastern suburbs swirl around me, shopping for clothes. I walk down a side street and into the commission estate. An old Vietnamese woman stands on her balcony watching the children play basketball in the car park. I keep walking straight ahead, avoiding looking at anyone. Three Polynesian boys sit around listening to rap on their sound machine, smoking cigarettes, passing a joint around. I cross the car park and walk up Phil's street.

I knock twice at Phil's door and call out for him. Phil, it's Ari. He won't open the door if he doesn't recognise the voice. I walk into his lounge room, sniffing the incense, the nicotine and the dope. A young woman in a black singlet and tight black pants is sitting on a pillow against the wall. She's out of it. A man has his arm around her and he offers me his hand when I come in. I shake it and sit down on a pillow opposite them. Ari, this is Barbara and Gary. I nod, take out a cigarette and light it. A slow reggae song is coming from the stereo and the walls in the small lounge room are covered in prints from Asia and from the Pacific. Maori prints. Indian prints. Koorie prints. There is also a framed poster of James Dean in *Giant*. The one in which he is smoking a cigarette, cowboy hat on, his feet on the dashboard. I look back at the couple opposite and the woman has nodded off. I try to start a conversation.

–Doing anything tonight, Phil? He isn't. He still hasn't slept from the night before, and his skin is bursting out in rashes and lines cover his face. I'm still coming down, man. He offers me a joint and I take in a deep drag. It rushes through my body and I sink deeper into my pillow. I hate making small talk during a drug deal but with Phil it is unavoidable. We talk a little more about going out, reggae bands which I know shit about and his upcoming trip to Thailand. I pretend to be interested in all of it. Gary doesn't help much. After a few attempts at talking, his mouth and lips trying to form intelligible words, he gives up and settles into a sleep next to his girlfriend. Phil gets up and goes out the back to get my deal. I look through the records and the CDs. Mostly reggae, a little bit of Cat Stevens and Led Zeppelin, a couple of twelve-inches, but I can't find anything I like. I settle for the soundtrack from *Altered States* and turn the volume up. Good music for the smackheads on the couch.

Phil comes back in and I follow him into his bedroom. I pass him the joint and jump onto his bed. He throws the two bags of white powder onto my stomach and I pick them up and look at them. It looks like a gram in each. I grab my wallet and give him a hundred dollars. The deal done, I'm eager to get out, but it would seem rude. I lie back and let him talk. He talks about India, about opium dens in Kashmir and he lightly brushes his hands across my thighs and under my T-shirt. He rubs my groin and balls but he's not turning me on. I don't move away until he tries to pull down my trousers. He doesn't mind. He moves away as well and searches under the bed for something, pulling out a tin box wrapped in an old T-shirt. Do you want to blast some now?

-I thought you were going to sleep.

-There's a band on this afternoon at the pub down the street. He mentions some Koori band who play awful country and western. Want to come? I refuse and tell him I have to go home soon. The good Greek boy, eh, he laughs and leaves the room. I don't really want to hit up but the dope is strong and making me lethargic. Something to pull me up would be good. I've already refused sex with him, so I figure I might as well share a hit. He brings back a spoon and pulls out two syringes, two swabs and a vial of sterile water. I get a little apprehensive looking at the gear. I don't blast shit often. It scares my friends.

He hands me his belt and I tie it around my forearm. From his bedside table I pick up a large Buddha and use it to flex the muscles in my arm until I can see the veins appearing. Phil grabs a packet of powder from the tin box and asks me how much I want. It looks around two grams worth to me and I say a quarter. He nods and prepares the mixture. It's speed, not smack, and I know it won't kill me but I can't help feeling anxious. I see an image of my father coming in to find his son slumped dead over a needle. I wonder what would happen if the nerves linking my brain, my heart and my lungs malfunction and the drug bursts my body apart.

Phil takes my arm and I watch him feel for a strong vein. He punctures the skin, I don't feel any pain, and I watch a few drops of blood enter the syringe. He pushes the liquid through the needle and into my vein and I loosen the belt. He hands me a swab and while I'm brushing the antiseptic onto the puncture the drug jumps into my brain. My skin, my hair are charged with electricity and I can feel every cell in my body form myriad patterns. My inner body becomes a kaleidoscope. The rush dissipates, I remove the swab and get to my feet.

–Feeling good? asks Phil. Feeling good, I answer and stand still for a moment, trying to regain some balance. I grow conscious of the music on the stereo and concentrate on the discordant electronic notes. I walk into the bathroom and look at my eyes, my face in the mirror. The skin seems to be stretched back, following the contours of my skull. I look thin, and I brush my fingers along my stubble. I can feel every hair. In the bedroom Phil is shooting up and I wait for him to finish, then help him clean up the mess. I stick my two grams worth of drugs in my cigarette packet and wave Phil goodbye. He lies on the bed, playing with his cock. He says *ciao* and asks me to get him a cigarette. I throw him one of mine and get out of the place quick. Outside the sun is white hot, reflecting off the car bonnets and making the street shimmer. I jump into the sunshine and light a cigarette. I look down at my vein. A clean hit. You can hardly tell.

Speed is exhilaration. Speed is colours reflecting light with greater intensity. Speed, if it's good, can take me higher than I can ever go, higher than my natural bodily chemicals can take me. Speed, they say, is cheap shit; putting amphetamines mixed with Ajax up your nose, in your veins. Speed, my friends and the drug handbooks they give you in school say, and the people on heroin say, is cheap, nasty. Good high, terrible low.

I say speed is exhilaration. I walk up Lennox Street to Bridge Road and the Pelaco factory where Mum used to work shines harsh white against a luminous blue sky. Speed is extra pumps for my heart, the drug grabs me by the throat and reaches down for my balls. On speed I like to stand under the shower for half–an–hour, just after the effect has come on, feel the water belting me.

On speed I like to fuck. Fucking with lots of touching. Feel every hair on their body, on my body. On speed I want to enclose myself in folds of warm, vibrating skin. On speed I want to penetrate. On speed, when my dick is soft, it is wrinkled and petite. Erect, on speed, all the blood in my body seems to rush and meet at one point, pulsate at one point. I can push it through my clenched fist, a tight sphincter. No pain, just exhilaration. Speed is exhilaration.

On speed I feel macho but not aggressive. I'm friendly to everyone. Speed evaporates fear. On speed I dance with my body and my soul. In this white powder they've distilled the essence of the Greek word *kefi*. *Kefi* is the urge to dance, to be with good friends, to open your arms to life. Straight, I can approximate *kefi*, but I am always conscious of fighting off boredom. Speed doesn't let you get bored.

Coming down off speed requires preparation. You feel the headache beginning, the jaw hurts. And time stands still. Sitting in the lounge room slowly looking through photo albums, it seems it takes an hour for the cigarette to reach the ashtray, an hour for it to come back to your mouth. I drink lots of water, try to piss, try to enjoy what's happening to my body. Experiencing the body as if it is working in slow–mo. Coming down I masturbate, lying in bed, the sheets and blankets at my feet, watching myself wank. In slow motion. Using lots of spit or Vaseline or baby lotion or Mum's face cream. Take it slowly, my dick feeling raw, sore, and when I blast, the headache, the sore jaw, the clenched teeth, all the pain of coming down explodes out of my body through my dick. Out in the drops of come falling on my chest, on the sheets. I don't move for five minutes, ten minutes, half-an-hour, let it dry in white crystal patterns across my naked body. Enjoy the release; then get up, take a piss, snatch one or two or three of Dad's Valiums and fall slowly asleep.

I'm walking down Lennox Street, the Pelaco sign burning into my eyes. I feel so high that I feel I can touch that sign. No boredom, just exhilaration.

My perfect tape

My perfect tape, the tape I listen to the most, is two years old. A collection culled from my records, Peter's records, friends' records. Side A: *I Want You Back*, Jackson 5; *Lost in Music*, Sister Sledge; *Little Red Corvette*, Prince; *I Got You*, Split Enz; *Everything She Wants*, Wham; *Broken English*, Marianne Faithfull; *Gimme Shelter*, Rolling Stones; *Funkin' for Jamaica*, Tom Brown; *Cloudy Sunday*, Sotiria Bellou. Side B: *Living for the City*, Stevie Wonder; *Temptation*, Heaven 17; *Walk Away Renée*, Four Tops; *Going Back to Cali*, L.L. Cool J; *Legs*, ZZ Top; *Man in Uniform*, Gang of Four; *Walk This Way*, Run DMC; *Like a Prayer*, Madonna; *The Road*, Manos Loizos. Not necessarily my favourite songs, not a tape I planned. A tape I put together over several days. But it has become my soundtrack to happiness. A soundtrack that goes nicely with speed, with summer.

Little sister

Little sister, don't you do what your big brother done. When I get home Dad has gone to the coffee shop, Mum is talking to her sister on the phone and Alex is dancing to Elvis

Presley in the lounge room. I move around her a little, then
lift her up high till she can touch the ceiling and give her a
big kiss on the cheek. She looks right into my eyes and
grins. Brother flying high, is he? I nod and she continues
dancing. I wait till the song playing has finished and then
put the needle onto 'Little Egypt'. I sit on the couch and
watch Alex dance to the song through half-closed eyes. This
is my favourite Presley song.

Mum comes into the room. I can remember when this
song came out, she says, sounding like she is bragging. As
if I care. If she had written the song, or performed it, that
would be a different matter. She joins my sister in the dance
and I start giggling uncontrollably. They both dance well,
gyrating their hips and waving their arms, doing a *tsiftiteli*.
I'm going to have a shower, I say, and grab a towel and my
radio from my room.

The hot water on my body gives the speed high a second
rush and I sing along to whatever song comes on the radio.
When I'm finished washing I brush my teeth in the shower
and piss into the drain. My cock is shrivelled. I try to get a
hard-on but I'm too high. Instead I do some push-ups and
sit-ups in the bathroom. When I'm finished I look at my
naked body in the mirror. I'm in alright shape, my legs are
good, but I could do with some tightening up around the
stomach. I do a few more sit-ups then brush my hair back
with some coconut oil. The speed flushes through my body
in another wave and in the mirror my eyes shine, my lips
tremble.

I lie on the bed in my room and smoke a cigarette
listening to soul on the radio. I put the volume up loud to
drown out Alex's music in the lounge. I can't lie down for
long and jump up and try on two or three T-shirts for the
night out. I end up choosing a plain white T-shirt, put on
some jeans. I keep putting on and taking off a black vest,
looking at myself in the mirror from every angle to see what
I look like. Side on I prefer the T-shirt without the vest.

Front on the vest looks good on me. I end up taking off the vest and putting a badge over my right tit. Felix the Cat. A seventies disco number by Aretha Franklin comes on the radio and I turn it up as loud as I can without distortion. Mum bangs on the door and tells me to turn it down. I peek out my door and ask her if she feels like a whisky. She shakes her head, then smiles and goes off to the kitchen. I comb my hair into shape and go out into the lounge room.

–Why are you wearing that stupid badge? I ignore Alex and go grab my whisky and sit down in the kitchen with Mum. What are you going to do tonight? I ask her.

–Depends if your dad comes home early from the *kafenio.* Maybe we'll visit your aunt. I cradle the glass in my hand. It bothers me that Mum has to wait for Dad before she goes out, as if she's not an adult and can't make a decision on her own. But she won't listen to me so I decide not to push the issue. I think you should go on your own, is all I can say. She touches my hand and takes a hit of whisky from her glass. What are you up to tonight?

Dumb question. She knows I'm only going to sketch in a few details for her. I'll go out with Joe, meet some people. I change the conversation.

–Mum, I want to go to Greece.

–With what money? Hers and Dad's, of course. I don't have any. But I don't say that.

–With whatever I can scrounge up. Don't you want me to go? Dad would want me to go.

–Your father would want to go with you. She pours herself another drink and lights a cigarette. I grab one from her pack. Mum, I've been thinking about it. I'd really like to go, don't you want me to go?

–Of course I'd like you to go. But when, how, where you going to get your money, *manoula mou?* You have to get a job first. I'm not put off by her mentioning work. I'm enjoying our chat. When I'm speeding, when Mum's drinking, we can converse like normal people, without getting heated and uptight with each other.

–Mum, there's no work here. Maybe I can get work in Greece. My mother looks sad. Please, Ari *mou*, don't say that. I don't want the family to split up. I couldn't stop worrying if you were in Greece forever. It wouldn't be forever, I answer. I cannot envisage forever, I'm thinking more a couple of years living in a different country, meeting new people, getting excited about unfamiliar sights, sounds and smells. Also a couple of years away from the family and all their hang–ups and expectations. I can't say that of course. It wouldn't be forever, I answer. Just a year or so.

–Ari, why don't you go back to school. You are going to be twenty next year. An adult and you still don't have a plan for your life.

I butt out my cigarette and sit back in the kitchen chair looking at my mother. I don't know what to answer her. I could go back to school, I could try and get some shit job cleaning toilets in a hospital somewhere, or disappear in some office labyrinth in the city somewhere, doing a job that a computer could do faster and better than me anyway. A computer wouldn't have an attitude problem. I try to put some words together, and though I know what I want to say, I can't make my lips move. I don't want a life like she has. And I don't want the life she wants for me. I hear Alex in the next room trying to find a song on an old record. She lands the needle on the vinyl with a small scratch. If you're going to play my records, take care of them, I yell at her. She ignores me and turns up the volume. Mum finishes her glass and gets up, humming to the song. Tom Waits. I sing along with her. I sit on the kitchen bench and take up the telephone, dialling and listening to my mother sing in her deep tone, and Alex's voice, shrill in the background.

–Australeza, I tease my mum. She hits me lightly across my legs. Wog, she calls me.

It is night outside

It is night outside the kitchen window and with the warm whisky in my stomach, the speed in my veins, I'm keen to move from the house and into the big world outside. Joe sounds half-asleep on the phone so I keep the conversation short and simple. What time should I come over? I ask. Ten, he says. There is a pause. Dina is coming as well. Fine, I say. I don't feel fine about it. It means that she'll bring along some dumb cousin and we'll have to end up going somewhere woggy. Where do you want to go? he asks me.

–Hold on. Alex, I yell. My sister comes into the kitchen. Where are you going tonight? She mentions some club in Brunswick. We'll drive you, I tell her, and get back to the phone. How about the Retreat? I say. Joe's voice picks up. Yeah, good idea, he says. He's scared I'm going to introduce Dina to faggot joints in the inner city and open her mind. I'm not interested in expanding Dina's mind at all, but I'm concerned that Joe is closing off his. A distant laugh comes from the receiver. Who's there? No one, Joe replies, Mum and Dad are watching a Greek movie. Some shit comedy. Okay, I say, see you at ten. I start dialling immediately. Mum, I say, watching her prepare a salad, there's a Greek movie on TV. I've seen it, she says, looking a little unsteady on her feet. Watch the knife, I say to her. She's cutting thin slices of tomato and she's on her third whisky.

–Who is it? A gruff voice is on the phone. Hello, *theo*, this is Ari. Mr Petroukis is pissed and he asks me three or four questions without waiting for my answer. Got a job yet, Ari? is his final question. No, and you? I ask. Mr Petroukis is unemployed as well. His laugh is loud and rings clearly down the line. I can almost feel the spittle spraying against my cheek, can almost smell the cigars and wine on his breath. No job, no job, Ari, he says in English. His laughter stops and now his voice is sad. Fucked up country, fucked up country. He continues repeating words in English. He is moaning. Is Yianni there? I ask, not wanting to listen to his maudlin thoughts. Sure, Ari *mou*, sure. He calls his son and I whisper to Mum that Mr Petroukis is drunk. Good idea, she says and goes to pour herself another shot.

–Darling, how are you? Johnno sounds in a good mood. Good, I answer. All our parents are getting pissed tonight.

–At least your mother can hold her liquor. My old man's off his tits.

–Put him to bed, I tell him. Johnno laughs. That stinking body, no way. I'm going to point him towards the shower in a moment and then he'll head off into the night looking for a good fuck. Some divorced mama with dyed blonde hair or some dumb fag looking for a rough Greek fuck. I hear Mr Petroukis yelling abuse at his son. Johnno tells him to fuck off in Greek.

–Want to meet up tonight, I ask.

–Yes, later. Toula's being taken out to dinner. Toula is Johnno's drag name.

–My boss's brother-in-law is showing me the town tonight. Johnno works part-time in a sex shop and his boss is a weedy-looking Croat with no hair and no teeth. Is this guy Croat as well? I ask.

–Yes, sighs Johnno. A dreamboat. Hairy all over, a big gut and big muscles. He giggles. I'm hoping he's big all over.

I hear Mr Petroukis abusing his son. Johnno lets out a stream of Greek. Go-fuck-yourself-you-drunk-as-fuck-animal. I look up and my mother has finished the salad and is looking at me, shaking her head. I start laughing, enjoying the argument I'm listening to on the other end of the phone, enjoying the music Alex is playing, enjoying the drugs in my system.

–Johnno, I shout, Johnno, we'll meet at1.30 or there-abouts.

–Sure, darling. What are you doing beforehand?

–Going out with Joe and his girlfriend to the Retreat.

–God, maybe I should come. Toula hasn't made an appearance there for a while.

–Better not. Joe doesn't want Dina exposed to his degenerate friends. Johnno lets out a loud, high–pitched laugh. Don't tempt me, Ari, I might end up there and ask Joe for a dance. Do you think Dina will get jealous? Johnno in drag is pretty stunning but I want to keep him away from the wog crowd. I'm not looking for trouble with Joe.

–Meet you at 1.30 at the Peel, I say.

–No, meet me at the Punters, that's where the Croat wants to go after dinner.

–See you there. Johnno blows me a kiss over the phone and I put down the receiver.

Mum is looking for me and it's obvious I've done something wrong. Can I have a cigarette? I ask her. She gives me one and then keeps on staring at me. What is it? You know what it is, she says, why do you hang around that *pousti*?

–Because he's my friend.

–He's not a good friend to have. I leave the room and refuse to take up the conversation. All I say is, none of your business. She starts setting plates on the table, banging them loudly on the table top, and I go to talk to Alex. She's in her room getting dressed.

–You want to come out with us tonight? I ask her. She has put on a too–tight black polo–neck sweater and is sitting by her mirror applying make-up. She refuses. Can I be dropped off at Charlie's? I nod. Joe won't mind, I answer, and start flicking through the magazines on her bed. She catches my eye in the mirror. You got speed? she asks. Come into my room when you're finished, I say, and leave her to paint her face in shades of scarlet and turquoise.

In my room I lock the door behind me and take one

packet of speed from the Bogart and Bacall cigarette case.
It's a tin case, with a colour reproduction of the poster for
To Have and Have Not on the lid. Mum found it for me at
the markets and I keep my drugs in it. I pour a third of the
white powder onto the shiny jackets of an atlas and cut the
speed with my bank card, listening out for Mum. I divide
the powder into four small lines.

Alex knocks on my door and asks to come in. I open up
for her, then quickly lock it behind us. She's dressed
completely in black; tight black jeans and a black scarf
around her shoulders. She's gone sparse with the make-up,
her lips blood red, a faint trace of blue along her eyelids.
She doesn't look seventeen, she looks older than me and
she looks beautiful. I enjoy it when my sister looks attractive,
when my brother looks handsome. I am proud of their
beauty. It is as if it reflects glory back on me.

–You're looking sexy, I say, and hand her a small straw from
the cigarette case. Two lines for you, I say. She crouches
at the end of the bed and snorts the speed, one line for
each nostril. She's not a big drug taker, my little sister, and
she inhales the speed in short snorts, twisting her face, not
enjoying the powder burning through her nasal passage, not
enjoying the bitter taste at the back of her throat. She only
finishes half of the second line.

–Have a rest. She hands me the straw and I inhale the
three lines of powder in three quick snorts. Fetch me an
orange juice, I ask her, and I wipe the white residue off the
atlas and lick it off my hand. Alex brings a glass of juice for
me and she bites into a peach. The bitter taste in my mouth
goes away and the powder rushes along the back of my
head, teasing the hair on my neck. My cheeks are flushed.

Alex is breathing hard. Her brown eyes are dancing. She
takes two cigarettes from the pack on my desk, lighting one
for me as well. Do you like Charlie? she asks me.

–I don't trust him, I say.

–You don't trust Arabs. She's right. I don't trust Arab boys with my sister. Alex can do what she likes with boys, it's not my place to judge her, but she'd be stupid to fall for an Arab. Like Greeks, like any wogs, they don't have the guts to fight Mummy and Daddy.

–Just don't get serious, I say to her, that's what I worry about.

–And you, she asks, are you getting serious about anyone? I smell sweat, dry come. Think about George rolling a joint for me, sitting in the kitchen, touched all over by the rays of the sun.

–We're too young to get serious, I reply.

–You should come back to school and repeat final year. We could be in class together. I groan and take a big drag on the cigarette.

–Ari, you've got no initiative, she says. We look at each other for a moment and then burst out laughing.

–Get fucked woman, I giggle, you sound like a social worker. Mum knocks on the door. Dinner's ready, she says.

–I'm not hungry, Alex replies. I take her hand and lift her off the bed. Eat something, I say, you're too thin. Bullshit, she replies, and I can't eat now that I've had the speed.

–Just nibble something. Have a bit of salad. We walk out of my room. Arab boys like a bit of fat, you know.

Fried meatballs

Fried meatballs, bread, fetta and salad on the table. I eat more than I really feel like eating. To satisfy Mum. Alex picks at the salad and can only manage a couple of meatballs. Mum's stopped drinking alcohol and is sipping some water. It doesn't look like Dad is coming home in time for dinner and I can see she's getting tense. She keeps rubbing the vein on her forehead.

–Are you going to go to *thea's*? I ask. She doesn't say

anything. Go Mum, Alex says, what the hell are you going to do on your own on a Saturday night.

-My children could stay with me. Her eyes cloud over. My children could keep me company. Alex makes a face and gets up from the table. I don't want a lecture, she says, and goes off into the lounge. My mum gets up, follows her, and they begin an argument. I grab a magazine, one of my mother's, and flick through it. I hear snatches of the argument. Alex is too young to be going out. I read about a woman who is married to a man who bashes her. Alex says the house feels like a prison to her. Mum says she's worked hard all her life for us kids and we've all let her down. Alex yells at her that she should live her own life, not live through her kids. I put down the magazine and go to the bathroom to clean my face. I comb my hair, put some aftershave on my armpits. I grab my cigarettes, the speed and my wallet, and march into the lounge room. Mum is on the sofa crying. Alex is in her room. I take Mum's hand. Come on, we'll walk you over to *Thea* Tasia. Mum kisses me and gets up. She asks me to clear the table and to leave the meatballs and salad out for my father. I clean up quickly, putting plastic wrap over the leftover food, a towel over the bread and rinse the dirty plates and cutlery in the sink. When I'm finished Mum has changed into a white jumper, put some make-up on and has her little black bag under her arm. How do I look? she asks. Beautiful, says Alex. Sexy, I say to her.

The night is warm with a slight breeze that gently rolls over my exposed neck and over my face. The speed accentuates the lights and colours of the street, and the glow from one lamppost reaches over and meets the glow from the next; the air seems to hum from the electricity. I walk ahead of my mother and sister who are talking small talk. Two drunk boys walk past us. The smell of beer is strong on them. We leave Mum at my aunt's gate, and Alex and I walk down a side street to the tram stop on Swan Street. Two young women, in their early twenties, both in black stockings and floral patterned dresses are sitting waiting for the same tram. Alex and I sit on the brick fence of a dark cottage behind the stop. My sister asks for a cigarette and I scowl but hand one over. Can't you buy your own? I snap at her. She tells me to fuck off loudly and one of the women turns around and gives me a dirty look. A gold hoop hangs from her nose. There are some Anglo women who hate wog men, who cannot stand the sight of us, can't stand the smells we exude, the pitch of our voices, the sound of our laugh when we make a joke. They look at us and all they see is a hairy back, they see a wife beater. This hippie woman hates me and I play up to it. I look her up and down and then just stare at her. She turns to her friend and says something. Her friend turns around and glances at me. To her I give a smile. She doesn't smile back but turns away, ignoring me, snubbing me. I don't care. They've got nothing to do with my life.

Alex asks me the time and I glance at my watch. Nine o'clock. I look towards the city skyline, at the Dimmey's tower and the railway bridge across Richmond station, but no tram is visible, only the bright lights of cars. Across the road the Lebanese woman from the milk bar comes out to have a fag in the night air. She sees us and yells a hello. I salute her and Alex wanders over to share a cigarette with her. I'm alone at the stop with the two uptight women and I bang my feet against the brick wall in time with a beat in my head. The women are talking about a film they are going to see in Camberwell, a bad French film I've already seen. Two hours with a boring couple in Paris deciding whether to divorce or stay together. It didn't even include any good shots of Paris. It's not very good, I say to them. They ignore me. Fuck off then, I say under my breath. All I want is to make some conversation while waiting for the tram. I look back towards the city and I see a tram in the distance. Alex,

I yell across the street, the tram is coming. She says goodbye to the Lebanese woman and crosses the street. How's Sonia? She's okay, says my sister, she's on her own tonight because her husband is out gambling and Pierre's fucked off with his friends.

-She should just lock up the shop and fuck off as well. Alex nods in agreement. But you know what her old man is like, he'll fucking kill her if he finds out she closed shop early. Fucking Lebo men, my sister spits out. The woman with the hoop nose-ring turns around to us and nods agreement. What does she know about wogs, with her golden hair and milk-white skin. The tram arrives and we all board it, Alex and I moving to the back, the two women sit up front near the driver.

The tram is full of drunk cricket fans returning from the day's game. Alex is talking away at me, telling me gossip about her friends and I'm not very interested, I keep turning away from her, looking out the window at the passing shops. She doesn't care, she's just happy to talk. I glance at the women who were at the tram stop and they are obviously avoiding me and Alex. A wave of anger hits me. It's not like I've done anything wrong. Maybe they think my voice is too loud. I don't know what it is but they are filling me with a load of spite tonight and I'm tempted to do something stupid like harass them, wolf whistle them when they get off at their stop, do something to confirm all their worst impressions about me.

Across from me and Alex a man has fallen asleep, his legs outstretched, his T-shirt is a little too short and his belly is peeking out from above his jeans. A white, smooth belly. No stomach hairs at all. I get a hard-on staring at him. I join in the conversation with Alex to forget the women, and the man in front of me. The tram rumbles along its tracks. The man wakes up, rubs his face and looks at me. A casual glance and I stare straight into his eyes. He stares back, just for second, then looks out the window, reaches up, pulls the cord, gets up and stands by the doorway. I don't let myself look at him, but continue gazing out the window at the world going by. A few stops after he gets off, the two women get up. The tram stops outside the cinema and I notice a billboard advertising *The Grifters* John Cusack and Angelica Huston's faces reflected on the tram window. The women begin to dismount and I call after them, forget the frog movie, go see *The Grifters* The bitch with the nosering gives me the finger, but her girlfriend smiles at me this time. I settle back into my seat, pleased with myself, and Alex punches my shoulder. She likes you, she whispers to me. I say nothing; I don't give a damn. I just wanted some acknowledgment.

I saw John Cusack interviewed

I saw John Cusack interviewed on late-night television and he looked like me. Everyone else was in bed and I was waiting for the late movie to start. On 'Entertainment This Week', or 'Entertainment Now', or whatever they call it. He was talking about wanting to work on serious movies, not on pap, not on some computer-generated flimsy, and as he was talking I thought he reminded me of someone. He smoked a cigarette. I remember that, and his thinning hair was swept back. On Mum and Dad's bedroom drawer they have a black and white photo of me taken a few years ago, and I'm wearing a black jumper, smoking a cigarette and looking angrily at the camera. Peter had snapped the photo when I was in the middle of a fight with Alex. At the time I yelled and yelled at him for taking the picture, but it is one of the few photos of myself I can bear to look at. Maybe because, if you just looked at it, you couldn't tell when it was taken; this year, last year, twenty years ago. This photo could have been taken anywhere; it could be anyone. And it clicked, watching John Cusack getting interviewed, that he looked like me in this photo. Since then I've kept an eye out for his movies, even if they look like they may be shit. I've seen *The Grifters* many times. It is a Hollywood movie that doesn't feel like Hollywood, it feels like the people who made it cared for something else apart from drugs and money. And he was in *Say Anything*. In *Say Anything* he falls in love with this rich girl, who is avoiding him, and at dawn he stands outside her house, in a raincoat, holding a ghetto blaster high above his head. He's playing *In Your Eyes*, the Peter Gabriel song, to get her attention. One day I'd like to meet someone I felt so strongly about that I would get up at dawn to play them a love song. Not to worry about what the neighbours say, what his parents will say. I can't sing so it will be my own form of serenade. Then not only will I look like John Cusack, I'll be like John Cusack.

Jesus, I'd love to serenade John Cusack.

Alex pulls at my T-shirt. The tram is running down a large road and apart from the street lights, on either side of the highway houses stretch for miles and miles in darkness. I pull the cord and we get off at an intersection. There is a petrol station at each corner. The four of them are huge, all brightly lit, each with its own car park. The Shell, BP, Ampol and Caltex signs form a neon oasis at the centre of the dark flatlands reaching out from all sides of the intersection. I put a cigarette to my mouth, light it and offer one to Alex. She takes it and we cross the road, into the suburbs.

No one, of course, is on the streets. And every street around here looks like every other street, every stranger you meet walking along looks like the same stranger you passed blocks ago. The blocks are huge. Big brick buildings, one after another. This could be Balwyn, could be Burwood, could be Vermont. Could be Mitcham. Maybe if you grew up around here all the space might mean something to you. East, west, south, north, the city of Melbourne blurs into itself. Concrete on concrete, brick veneer on brick veneer, weatherboard on weatherboard. Walking through the suburbs, I feel like I'm in the ugliest place on the planet.

-I'd like a house around here. Alex stops in front of a concrete monstrosity, small lion statues on the gate and marble pillars on the front verandah.

-What the fuck for? I say to her. For somewhere to live where I don't feel crammed, she says. She starts reeling off a list of things she'd like in life. A big house, a big backyard, a dog, a good job. I don't listen, I just keep walking a little ahead of her, letting the drugs wrap themselves around my head and enjoying the night breeze. We pass an old couple walking their dog.

-You want to be like them? The old woman turns and looks at us. Shut up, my sister says in Greek. You want to be like them? I insist in English. You don't ever want to get out of this city, do something different with your life? She stops in front of another house and inspects the garden. I keep walking and she runs to catch up to me. We get to Joe's place.

The grass in the front yard is immaculately mowed and Dina, Joe and his sister, Betty, are smoking cigarettes on the porch. A faint trace of tobacco, marijuana and olive oil lingers among the plants in the garden. Alex sits down on a step and I kiss the girls hello, slap Joe on the back and go into the house. A bong sits on the lounge-room table, the television is on and the sound is down. A shit CD is playing on the stereo, some ugly white noise like Phil Collins or Michael Bolton. I stop the music, whisk through the CDs on the shelf and find an old Rolling Stones record. *Let it Bleed.* I program *Gimme Shelter* first, then *You Can't Always Get What You Want*, then *Love in Vain* and finish with *Midnight Rambler.* They are the only four songs I want to hear. I turn the volume up, have a bong and then join the others on the steps.

-Why'd you take the other one off? Dina is glaring at me. Joe has his arm around her and she's running a middle finger up and down his naked arm.

–Because it's shit. Betty laughs and claps her hands.

–Well, I think this is shit. I say nothing, just croon along to the chorus of *Gimme Shelter*. Give a fuck, I'm thinking, it's all just a shot away. Dina gets up, unsteadily, maybe she's had too much dope and goes in the house. Joe looks concerned.

–Be friendly, Ari. For my friend's sake I get up and follow Dina into the house. She's standing in the kitchen, by the sink, rinsing greasy remainders of food off the plates. What do you want? she says when she sees me come in.

–To say I'm sorry. I'm only playing four songs, when it's over we'll put your CD on.

–No, it's alright, I know my music is daggy. Like, right, you think I'm a dag, don't you? She turns off the water and turns to face me. You do, don't you? I don't know, is what I'm thinking. Dag? Is that the word? She's commonplace, in her too-tight red dress, her teased hair, the heavy black mascara, the little gold cross around her neck. Her problem is that there are thousands of women like her sprinkled around this city. There's probably three or four girls like her in this street. I can't say that to her, and I don't want to say that to her. So I just give her a weak smile.

–I don't think you're a dag. She smiles back but I don't let her off the hook completely. I do think you're a wog.

–So what, I'm proud of it. And what are you? I don't answer. I'm not a wog, I'm not sure what I am but I'm not a wog. Not the way she means. Mick Jagger's voice comes on rough and soulful, the opening verse to *You Can't Always Get What You Want*. Dina starts to sway to the song: she's enjoying being stoned to it.

–I like this song. Dina comes and stands next to me. It's the speed, pushing me out of myself, it's the drug high, the smoke from the bong helping me connect with this young girl beside me. I keep talking, enjoying the sensation of her shoulder pressed against my side.

–My brother gave me this record for my fourteenth,

maybe it was my thirteenth birthday. I didn't really like the Stones before. All I knew was *Satisfaction*, *Tattoo You*, the more recent stuff. But when I first heard *Gimme Shelter* it blew me away, I used to play that song over and over and over till even Peter got sick of it and told me he'd break it over my fucking head if I played it again. The cunt, and he gave it to me. I laugh to myself, remembering.

Dina moves away. I prefer Greek music, she says, and moves into the lounge room for a bong. I keep talking, following her, going on a speed rave.

–A few months ago I was in this pub, it was early afternoon, more a bar than a pub, and this guy behind the counter is looking through a stack of CDs. I asked him if I could choose one and they had this greatest hits collection by the Stones. And I asked him to put that on, and when *You Can't Always Get What You Want* came on I started singing and this guy behind the bar starts singing. I can't sing, ask Joe, I never sing. This guy couldn't sing either but we must have both loved the song. When it finished, I look around, and there's only a few other people in the bar, a couple of young people, some middle-aged men. Empty really, afternoon on a weekday, but every single one of us has been singing along. I figured we must all have memories of that song. That's a great song, Dina, one that makes you connect with strangers.

She's not listening, crouched over the bong and taking in the smoke in one gulp. I stop talking and wait my turn. I look around at the walls, full of tapestries. The biggest one is of a small village by a river and three women are dancing on the river bank while two goat herders are watching them. Another tapestry is of the Madonna and child. Another of two reindeer in a forest. The glass the tapestries are framed behind is dull from dust. Where have your folks gone? I yell out to Joe on the porch. Dina, coughing a little from the smoke, hands me the bong. This place stinks, she says, it smells like a bordello.

-Sure does. Alex is standing in the doorway looking at me smoke. You must be right off your face, Ari. I let the smoke stay down in my lungs for as long as I can stand it, then release it slowly. Want one? I ask her and hand her the bong. Joe comes into the lounge room and sniffs the air. He tells me that his parents are visiting family. Does it really stink, Ari? I nod again. Just bomb the place with air freshener before we go, my sister tells him, and she comes over to me. She leans over and whispers Betty wants some speed. I go to see Betty on the porch. Joe follows me.

-You both want some speed? I ask. Betty jumps up but Joe shakes his head. We'll go into my room, Betty says, and Joe calls out softly to not say anything to Dina. I don't reply.

I detest the East

I detest the East. The whole fucking mass of it: the highways, the suburbs, the hills, the rich cunts, the smacked-out bored cunts. The whitest part of my city, where you'll see the authentic white Australian, is in the eastern suburbs. A backdrop of Seven Elevens, shopping malls, gigantic parking lots. I was picked up by a guy once, he lived in this shit-hole suburb somewhere, Burwood or Balwyn or Bentleigh or Boronia, and I woke up in this strange man's bed, got up and made myself a coffee, went into the front yard, looked down the street and thought oh-my-fucking-god-is-this-America? I didn't feel sane again until I reached the corrosive stenches of the city. Lead and carbon dioxide in my lungs to make me forget the Disneyland I had woken up to.

East are the brick-veneer fortresses of the wogs with money. On the edge, however, bordering the true Anglo affluence, never part of it. The rich wog fortresses are the border towns between the stinking rich pricks and the vast expanses of bored housewives and their drugged-out children who populate the outer Eastern suburbs. The men, the greying men in their ugly business shirts, shuffle paper around all day, have guilty sex in toilets or at the brothels on the way to the station, and return home every night to drop dead in front of the television. Television rules. School, work, shopping, sex, are distractions to the central activity of the Eastern suburbs: flicking the channels on the remote control.

I have managed to snatch some pleasure in the East. Long family drives when I was still a very young kid, driving up to the hills and we'd play amongst deep green trees, a rainforest so beautiful that it looked like it came out of some lush dream. Later, there were long drives out of the city where we would cleave through the Eastern suburbs, drive down the long stretches of road. I would lie back on the passenger seat, music throbbing around me in whatever car we were, the continuous loop of brick-veneer houses forming a visual mantra. In a car where you can move through the suburbs but never walk out and be part of them, never to lose yourself in them, I feel safe. In a car is how I best appreciate the East. And I hate cars.

But these are only snatches of pleasure. In the Eastern suburbs Aunt Nikki lives, my mother's second cousin. She made it big, married a fat wog in real estate, and comes to visit once a year, on Mum's name-day, dressed in fur and covered with gold chains, rings and bracelets. In her house all the furniture is covered in clear plastic so no dust, no dirt will stain the evidence of her material success. Her husband stinks of alcohol, and her children look like Americans.

My cousin, Aleko, also lives in the Eastern suburbs. Not on the rich hills near the river, but out in the flatlands of suburban hell. I'm not sure how we are related; maybe his old man and my old man grew up in the same village. Aleko calls himself Alan and all his friends are skips. He grows his hair long, smokes bongs with his Australian mates, gets drunk every night. He has a sister and she's trying to be a skip as well. She dyes her hair blonde, sneaks out at night to fuck with the *Australezo* and refuses to speak the wog language, to retain the wog name. Their mother cleans the toilets at the local primary school and returns home to a small concrete shit-box, trapped between neighbours who she has to yell at to be understood – every fucking utterance a humiliation. Her husband lifts crates every day, and is bored out of his skull every night. He comes to visit my father every weekend to enter the old world of coffee shops and intimate dialogue. In the East, in the new world of suburbia there is no dialogue, no conversation, no places to go out: for there is no need, there is television.

For my Aunt Nikki, Alan and his family don't exist. And it is true, they don't exist. They are invisible to the rich wogs by the river. The wog community is a backstabbing, money-hungry, snobbish, self-righteous community. It has no time for losers or deviants. The peasant Greeks who have made their money working the milk bars, delis, markets and fish shops of Melbourne look down on the long-haired loutish Greek boy and the bleached-blonde sluttish Greek girl with disdain and denial. The denial is total. You are not me. We are not you. Fuck off. You don't exist.

Ethnicity is a scam, a bullshit, a piece of crock. The fortresses of the rich wogs on the hill are there not to keep the *Australezo* out, but to refuse entry to the uneducated-long-haired-bleached-blonde-no-money wog. No matter what the roots of the rich wogs, Greek, Italian, Chinese, Vietnamese, Lebanese, Arab, whatever, I'd like to get a gun and shoot them all. Bang bang. The East is hell. Designed by Americans.

Betty is a wog who wants to be black

Betty is a wog who wants to be black; a Greek nigger. Her small bedroom is full of posters and prints. A tour poster

for Public Enemy. Spike Lee. Lots of Rasta prints. The
Koorie flag. The only white woman on her wall is Madonna.
The only white man is a faded psychedelic print of Che
Guevara. Every time I see her room I think this woman is
going to drop out, that she's going to have to leave the
suburbs as soon as she's legal. Her parents will scream and
rant, tear out their hair, bash her around a little but they
won't be able to stop her. And good luck to her. I sit on
her bed, she lights up some incense and hands me a small
mirror for me to line up the speed.

She watches me cut the powder.

–It's good stuff, I say, and prepare two large lines for her
and one for me. She asks me how much I want for it. I think
about it for a moment. Twenty dollars. She searches through
her desk, finds two plastic ten-dollar bills and hands them
to me. I roll one up tightly and hand it over to her. She
snorts the powder quickly, makes a face and hands the
rolled-up ten back. I snort my line and give her the mirror
to lick off. Want some alcohol? she asks, and I agree. While
she's off getting me something to drink I search through
her bookcase for something to flick through. I settle for a
book on film, a general introduction to cinema, with lots of
photographs. Betty comes back with two glasses of whisky.
I take it and slowly turn the pages of the book in my hand
while we talk.

–Got a cigarette? I hand her one of mine and light one
up for myself. You coming along tonight? I ask her. She
shakes her head.

–I'm meeting friends in the city. We're going out to see
a band.

–Who's playing? She mentions some Sydney band. All
keyboards and samples. I'm looking at a picture of a man
in a limousine staring straight ahead of him while an anguished
woman is banging on the car window. *The Conformist* I've
seen the film years ago, as a kid, when it played on TV. I
remember the elegant sets, a long hall in which beautifully

attired men and women waltzed together. The lead actor had a beautiful face, strong and handsome, a masculine face. It was hard to tell how old he was in the movie. He could have been in his twenties, he could have been in his forties. I hadn't really understood the film. Something to do with Italian fascists in the thirties. But the images have stayed in my head; the women dancing together, a black car dwarfed by a blizzard, a woman stroking another woman's leg. Some images of the film have permanently entered my dreams. You should see this film, I say to Betty, and hand her the book.

–What's it about?

–It's a thriller.

–It's old, isn't it? I check the date in the book.

–It's seventies. But set during a war.

She gives me back the book. Ari, why are you hanging out with dumbfuck wogs?

I think about the question. Most people you meet are dumb fucks. Wog, skip, black, Asian. Who should I hang out with? I ask her. She doesn't answer me, instead she comes and sits down next to me and starts kissing me softly on my cheek. I don't respond much but I let her carry on. She rubs my crotch for a little while but I still don't respond and she stops. She gets up and asks for another cigarette. I'm not turning you on, right? I blush and say nothing. Would it turn you on if it was Joe doing it to you? she continues. I look at her. Her fleshy body, her long black hair, the sheen of her soft skin. We fucked a couple of times, when I was still at school. Drunk at a party. Her breath smelling of alcohol, her cunt pink and wet was bitter to taste; kissing her neck while I pushed my cock into her, my eyes closed thinking of boys. I came quickly and I licked her clit to make her come, wrapping my tongue around her, rubbing my face on her vaginal lips. The smell of my semen mingled with the smell of her juices. I'm getting a hard-on thinking about it.

I reach up to her and pull her skirt above her thighs and

massage her crotch, rub my thumb along her panties. She strokes the back of my head, pulling lightly at my hair. I close my eyes and I'm entangled in George's body, as I rub my face in Betty's crotch. I pretend her soft tufts of pubic hair are his hard, short bristles. I stop, let her skirt fall back against her legs and smile at her. You're right, I say, I'd prefer you were Joe.

Betty raises her hand, stops for a moment, then slaps me hard across the face. I grab her hand and am about to twist it back, wanting to hurt her, to bruise her. Instead I stop, then start laughing. A deep speed laugh from the bottom of my stomach which is loud and infectious. Chill out dumbfuck wog, I manage to gasp through my laughter. Betty starts laughing as well and hugs me, we have tears in our eyes. Poofter, poofter, she giggles, choking on the words. She takes a drag from the cigarette, stops laughing at me, then looks serious. I'm glad you don't act like a faggot, Ari. The words ring in my ears. I flex my muscles. I'm a man, I say, in a deep drawl. And I take it up the arse. Of course you do, she answers, you're Greek. We all take it up the arse.

She finishes her whisky and then starts banging her hand against the bed. Like a metronome. One constant beat, singing softly to herself: I hate this fucking life, I hate this fucking life, I hate this life. Someone knocks on the door.

–Fuck off, she screams. A loud, piercing scream. Fuck off and leave us alone. Joe comes into the room, ignoring his sister. He talks directly to me. You shouldn't give her drugs, she gets out of control. She's just like Mum, he adds bitterly. Betty gets up and pushes against him. Get out, get out you prick. He slaps her around a bit and I stay sitting, holding the glass of whisky, waiting for the drama to finish. She calms down and takes hold of my hand. Come dance, she asks me.

–The others are here, Joe says, just get ready. We have to go. She ignores him. I follow her into the lounge. Dina,

Alex and two men and a woman I don't know are in a circle around the bong. I nod to them. Betty says nothing to them, doesn't acknowledge them. She goes over to the CDs and records and grabs a piece of vinyl and puts it on the turntable. A *tsiftiteli* comes on and she begins a slow belly dance. She motions to me to come and join her. I get up, but my steps are half-hearted, I'm a little embarrassed in front of the crowd of strangers. One of the men I don't know comes up and offers Betty the bong. She smokes it in the middle of the dance, and hands it to me to finish the smoke. I do.

The song ends, Joe takes the record off and introduces me to the others. A tall, stocky Italian boy called Arno, the woman, a Dina clone in a tight short skirt with teased hair, called Mary, and her boyfriend Stav, overweight, stinking of cheap aftershave. The introductions done Joe starts shutting up the house, emptying the ashtrays, putting the bong and the dope away, locking them in a box under his bed. He takes a can of air freshener from the toilet and begins to spray around the lounge, the kitchen, the hall, the couches. A nuclear blast of chemical perfume. Betty, Alex and I go out onto the porch, waiting for the others to join us. You're in for a real wog night, Betty says to me. I nod in agreement. She's right.

Alex skips down the stairs to the front yard and sways in the moonlight. She sings a Greek song and Betty joins her; they link arms on the lawn and dance around each other. Wogs, I yell at them. From across the road a neighbour yells out for us to shut up. Shut up yourself you cunt, Betty screams out into the night. Dogs start barking. Alex and Betty keep dancing, singing loudly, the moonlight shining on their exposed arms and legs, on their faces. The rest of their bodies shrouded in their dark clothes.

–We'll meet you in Brunswick, Joe calls to Stav. I've got to drop off my sister and Ari's sister. Stav nods and he and his friends set off in a big blue Commodore. Dina goes with them. The rest of us pile in Joe's car and I take the front seat and start playing with the radio. A station is playing T–Rex. Louder yells Betty in my ear. Yeah, louder, screams Alex. Louder? Okay. How's this, and I turn up the volume till it tears at our eardrums. Joe turns it down a little and shakes his head but he joins in with us at the chorus.

We weave through dark suburban streets, get onto the freeway and I'm grinning from ear to ear, listening to the radio, listening to my friends sing along, out of tune, watching the headlights of cars, watching the suburbs drop away as we head into the city.

NORTH

You think you're so clever
And classless and free
But you're still fucking peasants
As far as I can see
A working class hero is something to be

John Lennon *Working class hero*

A junkie

A junkie has fallen asleep on the Flinders Street station steps. A young boy in an old black coat and jeans. His girlfriend, maybe it's his sister, she looks like him, has her arms around him and she's staring out at the traffic and the floodlit intersection. We drop Betty off at the corner and she joins a few punks and hippies hanging around, smoking, avoiding the police. I don't like her friends, Joe mutters, as we drive away.

-You've become pretty straight, haven't you Joe? Alex leans forward and fiddles with the dial on the radio. Joe doesn't answer her. I turn around and wink at my sister. We drive up Elizabeth Street, onto the Parade and into Parkville. The traffic is slow entering Sydney Road and I spend my time humming along to the radio and checking out the Greek and Arab boys hanging out in the cafes.

-Fuck, this place is full of Turks. Joe looks disgusted. We've hit the North, Alex replies. We pass the town hall and turn into the street where Charlie lives. Are you coming in? Alex asks and I turn to Joe. He shakes his head but I tell him to wait a second. He turns off the engine and tells me not to be long. Alex and I get out.

In the front yard a group of dark-haired, dark-skinned boys are hanging around a car, playing at being mechanics, waving torches over the engine. They greet Alex and I shake Charlie's hand. He introduces me around. Mum is inside, he tells Alex, go in and say hello. I don't like him ordering my sister around but she's made the decision to go out with him and there's not a lot I can do about it. My arm goes around my sister's shoulder. I feel protective of her with all these boys around.

His mum is sitting watching television and his little brother and sister are playing card games around her feet. Alex

introduces me. She gets up and asks if I'm hungry. The
smell of oil and spices I don't recognise is in the room. She's
a big woman, and a black scarf covers her hair. The room
is sparse; a couple of couches, a small table, the television.
A few photos on the wall. A small bureau near the doorway
is cluttered with junk from Lebanon, including a hookah.
Alex sits down with the kids and they include her in their
game. The mother isn't warm towards my sister, but she
doesn't ignore her either. She asks Alex to make her a
coffee and Alex gets up and goes through a doorway into
what must be the kitchen.

—You happy your sister with Lebanezo? I'm not ready for
that question and immediately answer yes, just to be polite.
But I'm not happy about it. I don't care who Alex dates, and
personally I couldn't give a shit what Charlie is, but I don't
think Charlie is going to settle for a Christian girl. Not that
Alex is religious, but I know that the Muslim boys treat
Christian girls like shit. And the main problem is family; the
divide is too big, too deep. Alex hasn't told my parents she's
with a Muslim. That's one point in Charlie's favour. He's
faced the family about it. Are you happy that Charlie's with
a Greek? I ask her.

—In Beirut my neighbours were Greek, she answers, when
I was a little girl. We all live together, Orthodox, Muslim.
We all friends. She doesn't mention the Catholics. She
doesn't say that she's happy about Alex being with Charlie.

—Here in this country, everyone hates everyone else.

—Alex is a good girl, I venture. I sound insipid. She agrees.
I shake her hand. I'm pleased I've met you, I say.

—Me too. Maybe one day I meet your mother, your father.
I smile weakly. Maybe one day. I'm not looking forward to
it. I yell goodbye to Alex and go out into the yard. You
coming to the Retreat? I ask Charlie. His friends cross their
arms and wait for his answer. Maybe, he says, maybe not.
Part of me gets angry at his dismissal of me, at the line of
boys looking at me with their arms crossed. Part of me

sympathises with him. Why would he want to go out to a
Greek club? I say goodbye and walk out to Joe's car. I hear
laughter behind me and I give them the finger. My ears are
burning.

–What's your sister doing with that jerk? Joe starts the
car, does a u-turn and we head back to Sydney Road. Where
did she meet him?

–Some party. I don't want to talk about it with Joe. He
doesn't push it, instead we drive in silence and he parks his
car behind the town hall. Anyone around? he asks me. I get
out of the car and take a look. Further back in the car park
a group of Turkish boys are smoking a joint, talking in their
own language.

–It's cool, I answer Joe.

–Have you got any speed left? he asks me. I hand him a
packet of powder and stay out while he fixes himself a small
line. The moon is nearly full, the night is warm. A light
breeze. A gentle night. The sound of traffic on Sydney Road,
the faint murmur of the bouzouki can be heard. I light a
cigarette and wait for Joe to finish. He puts a safety lock on
the wheel, hands me the drugs wrapped in a twenty and a
ten. Too much, I tell him, and give him back the ten. He
refuses it. You need it, dole bludger. I call him a wanker.
Don't tell Dina, he orders me, I told her I've cut out all drugs
except dope. Sure, I answer.

Two drunk Greek men are standing at the entrance to
the pub engaged in an argument. The younger man, in a
white shirt and thin black tie, is arguing about politics. The
older man, in a black jumper, is disagreeing with everything
the younger man is saying. He keeps pointing his finger at
the younger man, digging it into his chest. The sounds of
music, of shouting, of conversation come out into the street.
I follow Joe through the door and the room we enter is
crowded with people, smoke is everywhere. Large crowds
are seated around circular tables, eating, drinking and
smoking. Every available space is taken up with people

standing around shouting to be heard above the music.
Greek folk songs, the unmistakable sounds of the *clarino*
and the bouzouki. The band are performing on a raised
platform at the back of the pub. They're all young Greek
men except for a dark-haired woman banging listlessly on
the tambourine. Occasionally she sings. A circle of young
women are dancing on the dance floor, holding hands and
performing a *sirto*.

I can't take in everything at once. Familiar faces pop out
of the crowd, wink or smile at me. I smile back but continue
to follow Joe, keeping my eyes on his broad back. The noise
and the motion of the crowd in the small pub is too much
for me, and I want to take Joe's hand, let him lead me
through the mass of people and noise. But of course I don't
take his hand, he wouldn't let me.

Dina and the others have secured a small table near the
band. Joe takes the seat Dina has saved for him and I stand
at the edge of the table. Does anyone want a drink? I ask.
They all shake their heads except Joe. Get me a pot, he
yells above the music.

The old men are congregated around the bar, drinking
whisky, ouzo, or pot after pot of beer. Young men and
women push their way around the bulky bodies of the old-
timers, trying to find a space to order a drink from the
barman. The barman is fat with thin grey hair made wet
from sweat. A cigarette on his lips. His first priority is the
old men. When they are all satisfied, he turns to the young
people and asks them what they want. No particular order,
it is whoever he notices first, not who has been waiting the
longest. I squeeze against a huge man with a beard and wait
my turn. Someone taps me on the shoulder. It's Spiro, a
good guy, a friend of my brother's. I shake his hand warmly.

-Your brother's here, he tells me. We exchange banalities.
How's study? I ask. The same, he replies. More empty
phrases follow. This is a great place. Yeah. It's crowded. Sure
is. Greeks make some noise, don't they? Sure do. He stops

talking for a while and looks around him, his eyes settling on a woman across the bar. He smiles softly at her and she returns the smile. Then she looks away. He turns back to me and drops his voice to a whisper. Peter said you might have some speed. I answer in a normal voice, no reason to whisper in a pub as noisy as this one, how much do you want? I've got a gram. Can I have half? Too much trouble I tell him, I'll sell you the gram for sixty. He agrees and tells me he'll meet me in the backyard in twenty minutes. Where's Peter? I ask him. He points to somewhere near the exit. I nod and he moves away and finds a place next to the woman who smiled back at him. Spiro is tall, good looking, a good body. He doesn't have much trouble starting a conversation.

An older man, maybe in his forties, with a long, thick moustache is staring at me. He's opposite me on the other side of the bar. I don't avoid his eyes. A blue fishing cap sits on his head, and a faded yellow shirt is open to his navel. He's wearing a white singlet underneath. Coarse, heavy hair appears over the top of the singlet. His chest is muscled, his stomach is beginning to fall to fat. But his thick arms, strong, tense, hairy, are pure muscle. I drop my gaze but keep him in the corner of my eye.

Sensuality, the availability of sex, I feel it every time I am surrounded by Greeks. Not only Greeks; Latins, Arabs too. In small ways, even if you don't like the clothes they are wearing, don't admire the style by which they present themselves, everyone in this place wants to be seen, to be admired. A chain of flirtation is ever-present. My mouth is dry. I need a drink. The drugs are circulating through my body. My skin is alive in sharp bursts of electricity. My nipples are erect, my face is flushed, the hair on my naked arms is tingling. I'll have to dance soon, or fuck soon. The energy inside me is pushing against the confines of my body.

The barman gets to me. Whatcha want? I ask for a pot,

and for a whisky and soda. I watch him pour the whisky into a glass and notice he's only pouring me a short one. I raise myself on the bar and yell more whisky, in Greek. The man in the fishing cap looks up. The barman grimaces but pours another dose into the glass. He slams the drinks down hard in front of me and barks out five dollars. I hand him five bucks, wink at the fishing cap man who turns to ignore me and I move back to my table.

Joe takes his beer and I tell him I'm going to take a wander. He doesn't hear me, he's talking to friends. I weave through the dancers and the crowd and find my brother. He's with a crowd of Greeks from uni. He hugs me, slaps me on the shoulder and says hello little brother. Introduces me around. I don't take in the names. Someone offers me a cigarette and I take it, light up, and take a big mouthful of whisky. Peter's face is flushed and he is slurring his words. He looks drunk.

-Spiro's looking for you, he tells me.

-He found me.

-Any go? Yeah, I reply. Peter smiles a big grin. His little brother supplying drugs lends him attitude amongst the uni crowd.

-Where's Janet? I ask.

-Don't know, with friends. Janet hates wog crowds, they intimidate her. I'm not surprised she's elsewhere. I want to ask where George is, but I don't. Peter doesn't offer the information, not that he knows he should.

-Have you danced yet? someone asks me. I shake my head. They've only played *demotika* so far, I say, I want something heavier. Conversation happens, talk about uni, a bit of politics, who is fucking up who. I don't join in. I'm content to hang around the edge of the circle, listening in. A woman comes into the pub. Her black hair in rich, thick curls piled above her head. She's wearing a torn black T-shirt with a silk white vest over it. She's beautiful and she sniffs the air as soon as she comes in, taking in the smells of the pub. She sees me and rushes up to me.

–Ari, give me a kiss. I give Maria a kiss, I give her a hug. How you doing, good-looking? I say.

–I'm fucking full. The circle of men I'm in parts and she takes the centre, nodding at everyone but talking to me. I've been out to dinner with this new boy and he took me to a pasta place. The best cheese cake I've had in ages. I'm here to dance off the kilos.

–Is he with you? She shakes her head. No, I'm meeting Kosta here later. I laugh. Maria is never short for a date. I know, I know, she laughs, I'm a slut. The only decent Greeks have all been sluts. She pauses. Or poofters, she adds, and winks at me. I wink back.

–I'm going to get a drink, she asks, want anything? Later, I reply. I've got some quick, do you want some? Her face lights up. Darling, she screams, and hugs me. That'll get rid of the cheese cake. She takes my hand and leads me through a door in the back of the pub and into the women's toilets.

We lock ourselves in a cubicle, avoiding the looks we get from the women doing their faces at the mirror. I pour the last of the speed from one packet onto the toilet lid and add a small amount of powder from the gram I'm going to sell to Spiro. Maria crouches against the cubicle door and lights a cigarette. She watches me cut up the powder into two medium-sized lines. How much do you want? I ask her.

–One of those will be plenty. I snort my line and squeeze myself into the corner while she snorts her share. When she's finished I sit on the toilet seat and she sits on my lap, both of us waiting for the drug to come into effect. She begins to sing me a Greek song, her voice a distorted echo of the song the band are playing. I hum along with her, swaying her on my knees. A platonic serenade that we both enjoy. When she's finished her song I ask her about her date.

–He's a bit thick, she answers. I wanted to sing him a song at the restaurant and he requested Gary Glitter. Fuck.

Australian men don't have a romantic bone in their weedy bodies.

I don't often fuck with Greeks

I don't often fuck with Greeks. It is protection for myself. Someone may know a friend of my parents, or know an uncle. Greeks have big mouths and word can get around. When I was fucking with women it was not such a problem. No one cared about what woman you slept with, it made you more a man, as long as you didn't end up getting someone's sister or someone's daughter pregnant. Fucking with Greek men is half sex, half a fight to see who is going to end up on top. When I get the urge to have sex with a dark man, a Mediterranean man, I end up in Coburg or Preston looking for Turkish or Lebanese cock, someone outside my community, someone no one I know is ever going to meet. Sometimes, however, I see a Greek man, not necessarily someone particularly handsome, and I want to feel their body against me, to use dirty Greek words with them, to have them whisper Greek obscenities.

When Maria and I get out of the women's toilets, the man in the fishing cap is waiting there. He doesn't say a word. I watch him walk out through the screen door into the pub's backyard. I tell Maria I'll catch up with her later and follow him.

Outside, the smells of beer mix with the stench of garbage. A group of four men are huddled together sharing a joint. The man in the fishing cap walks past them, out the open back gate and into the small car park beyond. I follow him in the night air, down a suburban side street. He glances back, then keeps on walking. He turns into an alley and I hesitate. I think of mad fuckers, think of my throat being slit, think of those crazy men who get off on death. The visions of madness entwine with my urge to have sex. Blood and semen; these days the liquids go together. I turn into the alley, slowly, walking into the dark landscape of a dream.

He is pissing, a thick stream against the boards. I come up next to him, unzip, take out my dick, conscious of it looking small and shrivelled from the speed. I don't pretend to piss, I stand next to him masturbating until I get a hard-on. He finishes pissing, plays with his thick dick, watching me from the corner of his eye. I look down at his cock and reach for it. He groans, a slight murmur. I smell piss, smell alcohol on him. I masturbate him and try to guide his big hairy hand onto my cock. He resists. Instead he pulls down on my shoulders and I squat and take the head of his cock in my mouth. I taste drops of urine. He thrusts against my throat and I keep pulling on my cock, trying to avoid getting on my knees because of the piss on the ground.

I'm off-balance and I try to get up. He pulls down harder on my shoulders. Don't spill any of it, he whispers savagely in Greek. I don't want him to come in my mouth, I fear the disease that might be floating inside his body. But he pushes his cock hard into my throat. I'm caught between two desires, to gorge on his cock, to take him inside me as deep as he can go, or to get up on my feet, push him against the wall and hurt him for debasing me.

Time, time betrays me. Before I can make a decision I feel the hot sting of liquid in my mouth. He pulls away and I spit out his semen, his stench from my mouth. He dries his cock on a handkerchief, zips up and starts to move away. I'm up on my feet, I grab his arm and push him against the alley wall. I stick my hard cock into his hand. Pull me, I bark out in Greek. He groans, but I have one arm against his chest, holding him back and he doesn't turn away. I hate him now and I don't let him leave. My cock feels like iron. He pulls at it and I look into his eyes, two shining glints of light in his dark, unshaved face.

He looks pained now, the strength I saw in him, the strength which attracted me to him, is spent; spilt on the ground, diluted in the urine. I keep watching his eyes, not allowing him to turn his face away. He hates what he's doing, feels no desire as he mechanically pushes my foreskin across my cock. I rub my free hand inside his shirt, weaving my fingers in the hair of his stomach and chest. I feel that I'm about to come. I lift his shirt above his nipples and my white flashes of sperm land on his stomach and down around his feet. He pushes me away, wipes himself and glaring at me tucks in his singlet. I spit into my hand and wipe my cock. He walks back to the pub and I lean against the wall and light a cigarette.

My breathing seems loud to my ears. I allow the night breeze to tease my body, to cool me down, and I piss against the alley wall. I tuck my T-shirt into my jeans, tread on the cigarette, mixing the tobacco in with the come and piss on the ground and walk back through the car park and into the backyard of the pub.

Spiro is waiting for me. My brother has his arm around a tall, beautiful woman in a black sweater and a short skirt. Her painted face is pale white, her curls tight and black as night. This is Ariadne, Peter introduces me. I shake her hand, I smell expensive perfume. Just a touch; a pleasing scent. I pull the packet of speed from my pocket and offer it to Spiro. He winks and slips sixty dollars in my hand. He hardly looks at the amount of powder in the bag. He trusts me. In the pub the band have begun to play *rembetika*. I sway to the music.

–You enjoy dancing. I nod to Ariadne, though it doesn't sound like a question. She can see I like dancing. This is a beautiful song, she continues. *Bring me a flagon of wine so I can forget the pains that poison my life.* We Greeks embrace our pain, don't we? She looks around at the three men standing before her. Shall we dance? She grabs my brother's hand and leads him inside.

–Who is she? I ask Spiro. He laughs and tells me she is the woman who is breaking Peter's heart. Janet, rough, large.

I think of her. Think of not seeing her again if Peter splits from her. There is nothing painful in my thoughts. Janet is Peter's business, not mine. Part of his life, nothing to do with mine. Spiro hands me a set of keys. Meet me upstairs in the storeroom he tells me, there's someone I want you to meet.

He walks off and I go inside and up the staircase which opens up into a dingy little room piled high with boxes of canned food and alcohol. A small wooden table and three wooden chairs. A full ashtray, tobacco papers, a deck of cards and two empty glasses sit on the table. I take a seat, rest my head on my arms and listen to the music downstairs. I remember a movie I saw on late-night television a long time ago. Gene Hackman locked in a room very much like this one. In the movie he was drinking. I feel like a drink.

I search the room. Behind a pile of boxes I find a half-drunk bottle of whisky. I fill one of the glasses and sit down, pretending I'm not in Brunswick, Melbourne but in some room in Chicago somewhere. There is a knock on the door, the pretence is shattered and Spiro comes in, a blonde girl behind him holding his hand. A thin Greek boy behind them. Spiro locks the door and makes the introductions. Ari, Kristin, Stephen. Kristin smiles at me. Stephen looks nervous. She is wearing a long hippie dress, each ear has three earrings, an Indian scarf is tied around her hair. Stephen is dressed in a dark grey op-shop sixties suit over a white shirt. A navy tie is tied loosely around his neck, his top button undone. Black sneakers on his feet. His face is marked by spots, he is uneasy, nervous. His eyes large and dark. He is beautiful and I avoid looking at him.

–Are you at uni? Kristin takes a chair next to me. No, I tell her. Ari is Peter's brother, Spiro tells her. I like your brother, she tells me. I don't answer. I don't care.

–Are you studying? Stephen sits on a crate. I don't study, I don't work, I tell him. He is about to ask me another

question, then decides against it. Spiro is emptying most of
the speed onto the table.

 –So what do you do? This woman won't leave me alone.
Whatever I like, I tell her. Spiro laughs. How old are you?
she continues. Nineteen, I answer, twenty in a few months.
I'm a Leo, I add. She whistles, dangerous, and smiles at me.
I smile back. Stephen lights a joint and passes it to me.

 The smoke is good. The others talk among themselves
and I listen in. Spiro arranges the speed into eight identical
lines. We each take a turn to snort our share. The three
thank me in turn. I take ten dollars out of my wallet and
hand it to Spiro. What's that for, man? he cries. For my
share, I answer. He refuses it but I'm persistent. I'm enjoying
being in the little room, away from the crowd and I'm sorry
I short-changed him on the gram. Buy me a drink downstairs,
I add, and he pockets the note.

 Stephen and Spiro start talking in Greek and Kristin enters
in the conversation with them. I'm surprised, she doesn't
look Greek. She hesitates over particular phrasing but her
spoken Greek is better than mine. More confident. I listen
to her voice, it is melodic. Stephen is berating her, his tone
pushy and angry as the subject moves to politics. Spiro
pours himself a glass of whisky, and like me, watches the
faces of the two young people arguing, occasionally winking
at me. I'm happy to sit here, intoxicated by the drugs, the
drink, and the beauty of the faces around me.

 –Marxism is dead, Kristin tells Stephen. He bangs his fist
on the table and stands over us.

 –Communism, the degenerate state of the Soviet Union
may be dead, but not Marxism. He looks around at me and
Spiro for support. I avert my eyes. He's talking politics and
I'm thinking how hot he looks.

 –Marxism, he continues, is not dead, it can't be dead. It's
the only theory that makes sense of alienation.

 I pour myself another drink. I'm not following the
conversation which matters shit to me. I'm on edge. I want

to talk, say something clever but I have nothing clever to
say. Kristin raises her voice as she argues against Stephen.

-Marxism led to the gulags. Stephen shakes his head.
That's bullshit, he explodes. He has eyes that are frightening.
He has eyes that burn. Greek eyes.

-That's your answer to everything isn't it, Kristin yells.
Something Stephen said has made her furious. Spiro touches
her shoulder and she pulls away. As someone who supported
communism don't you feel any responsibility for the failures
of communism? she continues.

-No. Stephen's voice is calm. No responsibility at all. He
pauses. Spiro is whistling a Greek tune. I'm feeling the speed
run down the back of my throat. Stephen turns to Kristin
and says, simply and quietly, no anger in his voice, I'm never
going to stop resisting capitalism.

-I resist it as well.

-Then give me a fucking solution to it. Stephen's spit falls
in a spray over Kristin, over me. Until you give me a solution
better than Marxism I remain a committed Marxist.

I get up, drink the remainder of my glass. I'm going
downstairs, I say, and fill the glass again. Kristin and Spiro
nod to me but Stephen's face is impassive. I want to say
something to him, but I am intimidated by the language he
uses and instead turn, unlock the door and walk out into
the hall. The sounds from downstairs rush into my ears, the
wail of the bouzouki, the sounds of shouting. The whole
pub is in a frenzy of motion. I breathe in the excitement
echoing off the walls and I am glad to be free of the more
intimate intensity of the small room. Stephen's eyes, dark,
angry. I am glad to escape.

Walking down the stairs, heading back to the singing, the
dancing, the conversations, I start a refrain in my head.
Singing along to the thirties hashish song they are playing
downstairs, I sing fuck politics, let's dance. I sing it in a Greek
accent, give the phrase middle-eastern inflections, draw out
the words and my voice reverberates on the vowels. Fuck

politics, let's dance I sing coming down the stairs. I'm angry
and I don't know what I'm angry about.

A Serbian guy lied to me

A Serbian guy lied to me the other day. I was sitting on a
bench at North Richmond station, waiting for a train to the
city. I had the Walkman on and was listening to the radio.
They were playing *Love Song*, an old Simple Minds song.
A young guy, stocky, unshaven and wearing cheap department store clothes sat next to me. I avoided him, he was
avoiding me. When the song finished I turned off the
Walkman and rustled through my bag looking for a tape to
play. The man turned to me and asked, in broken English,
sorry does this train go to Jolimont. Yes, I answered, took
off my earphones and asked him where he wanted to get
to. He had an interview for a cleaning job in some small
hotel in East Melbourne. The sun was shining, I was feeling
pleasant. I kept asking questions. Were are you from?
    –Greece, he answered. I looked at him, his skin was olive
but his hair was dirty blond, his eyes clear blue. Which part?
I said, in Greek.
    –Sorry, he replied, blushing, I'm Greek but I don't speak
Greek. I nodded at this, and put the earphones back. Bullshit
was what I was thinking, but bullshit is everywhere. I lie to
strangers all the time. I can understand not giving too much
away.
    I started the tape and I was swaying to the sweet harmonies
of the O-Jays. The man beside me tapped me on the
shoulder. I stopped my machine and I was back at North
Richmond station. Yeah, I demanded, aggressively. I'm not
really from Greece, he told me. I didn't answer. I'm from
Yugoslavia. I did not respond.
    –I'm Serbian.
    I scowled at him. I didn't know why he was persisting.

-Sometimes, he continued, if I tell people I'm Serbian they are not very happy. Sometimes they blame me for the war in Yugoslavia. Politicians are to blame for war, I answered. He laughed. The train was approaching, I said good luck with the job interview, put on my earphones and went into a different compartment.

The O-Jays were singing *Backstabbers*. They smile in your face. The Serb hates the Croat who hates the Bosnian who hates the Albanian who hates the Greek who hates the Turk who hates the Armenian who hates the Kurd who hates the Palestinian who hates the Jew who hates everybody. Everyone hates everyone else, a web of hatred connects the planet. A Cambodian woman across the aisle was trying to get her kid to shut up. I smiled at her and she smiled back. And the O-Jays were singing *They smile in your face, all the time they want to get your place*. Pol Pot was right to destroy, he was wrong not to work it out that you go all the way. You don't kill one class, one religion, one party. You kill everyone because we are all diseased, there is no way out of this shithole planet. War, disease, murder, AIDS, genocide, holocaust, famine. I can give ten dollars to an appeal if I want to, I can write a letter to the government. But the world is now too fucked up for small solutions. That's why I like the idea of it all ending in a nuclear holocaust. If I had access to the button, I'd push it.

As we got into Princes Bridge station I was imagining the apocalypse. I was getting so excited it was making my dick hard.

On the dance floor

On the dance floor my brother is swaying clumsily, self-consciously. He hasn't drunk enough to give himself over to the *zembekiko*. Ariadne is dancing with him, making no elaborate moves so as not to embarrass him, but even restrained her dancing is sensuous, her falls and twirls graceful; she moves in time with every painful note the band is playing. I watch them, a little embarrassed for my brother. I move to Joe's table and he asks me where I have been. Around, I tell him. Dina is pissed and holding on to his arm. We haven't seen you all night, she accuses me. Then, unexpectedly, she jolts, springs up and offers me her mouth to kiss. I kiss her gently on the lips, a kiss over in a second, but her lips feel soft against mine, warm. I sit beside her and she clutches my arm.

–Joe won't dance with me, she pouts. Joe doesn't do Greek dancing I answer.

–I know. She turns to her boyfriend and hits him hard on his chest. You should learn, she tells him in Greek. Joe, stoned, not drunk, because he is driving, gives her a smile and a long kiss. I turn away and Arno asks if I'd like a drink. Joe and Dina continue being affectionate to each other and I try to have a conversation with Stav and Mary.

I ask if they're enjoying the night. They both nod in unison. Stav leans over and shouts in my ear, I hear you're looking for work. Mary leans over as well. No, I answer, I'm not looking for work. Together they lean back. Stav leans forward again and I look at Mary to see if she's going to follow but she turns her head and watches the dancing. I'm studying commerce, Stav tells me.

–What's that? Mary hears, turns back to look at me. She seems angry. Stav is flustered. He tries to explain commerce to me but I'm not listening. The band have started playing a favourite song of mine. An old song of Tsitsanis, *Cloudy Sunday*, and the singer's seductive voice fills my ears. Stav's earnest words slip away, murmurs that cannot stop my enjoyment of the song. I ask them if they want to dance and they both refuse. I turn to Dina but she's in Joe's arms, her eyes closed, humming along. I get up and as I am about to jump on the dance floor Stav yells at me, Mary is doing law. Lawyers can't dance I tell him but they don't hear.

On the dance floor I move between bodies twirling and swaying to the pain of the music. But in our motions we transform the pain into joy. The speed lifts me above the other bodies and as the chorus is repeated for the last time I fall on one knee, jump up immediately, fall on the other, twirl, fall back on my knees and jump back into a standing position. The song ends quickly and I wipe a sweaty arm across my face and sit down. You're a good dancer, Stav tells me. I thank him. Arno arrives with the drinks and I swallow from my glass.

–Do you want to study? Arno has wide, round eyes that dominate his thin face. No, mate, I tell him, I don't want to study and no, I don't want to work. Joe gets up from the table. Ari, he says, you're a dickhead. I take another swallow of whisky. His words hurt me, there is a stab right down in my gut. The whisky reaches that spot and the pain diffuses. Joey, I answer him, you better apologise. He ignores me and heads off for the toilet. I get up and follow him.

–Fuck off. He spits the words at me. I keep following him, across the room into the toilet, and while he stands at the urinal pissing, I try to have a conversation. What have I done? I ask, trying not to plead, trying not to sound upset. He refuses to talk to me. He refuses to look at me. Someone flushes in one of the cubicles and I lower my voice and touch Joe on the shoulder.

–Man, what did I do, what did I do? Joe finishes his piss, shakes his cock, flushes and turns around to me. Grow up, fucking hell Ari, grow up. Get a job, I'm embarrassed to be seen with you. I study his face. Notice the light layer of fat forming under his chin, the small strands of wrinkles around the eyes. Get a life are his final words to me and he walks out of the toilet. A young boy comes up beside me and washes his hands at the sink. How are you doing? he asks in Greek. I don't reply, walk into a cubicle, close the door behind me, gather my fingers into a fist and smash into the cistern. The sound, a loud crash, reverberates around the cubicle. Mad motherfucker I hear the boy say and hear him leave the toilet. Alone, smelling urine, shit and cheap cologne, I spit into the basin. Fuck you, Joe, fuck you, you cunt. The words keep repeating. Fuck you Joe, fuck you, you cunt. I repeat them twice, three times, they become a chant. I breathe in deep, get out of the cubicle, comb my hair, check myself out in the mirror, run some water across my dry lips and go back.

I watch Joe leave the pub, Dina holding onto his hand: watching an ordinary man walk out with an ordinary woman into an ordinary life.

Joe's mother

Joe's mother went into hospital in our third year in high school. The woman flipped out, went crazy, took her Bible in one hand, an egg beater in the other, and roamed the streets of Burnley screaming that the Antichrist was coming. The news rushed through the school, there were whispers and jokes made in the locker rooms, in the *kafenio*, across the counters of the milk bars. My mother told me, and I listened wide-eyed, that the priest from the Burnley Street church tried to take her by the hand and she started pounding him with the Bible. My mother crossed herself as she told me.

In the school yard the story became embellished with adolescent lewdness. She had tried to stick the holy book in her vagina, had tried to proposition the priest, the priest accepted, they fucked on the altar. The simple story was that the woman had gone crazy. The embellishments were nursery horror stories to frighten the children and to keep the presence of insanity away. Joe's mother was normal, that was what scared everyone. An-eight-hours-a-day-factory-worker-with-two-normal-kids-and-a-fat-hard-working-wog-husband. The woman was so normal, a standard Greek wife heading towards middle age that her craziness affected everyone who knew her. The devil made her do it. That was the comfortable answer.

Joe's father kept everyone away, kept Joe and his sister away from school. I tried to call him and the phone was answered by his aunt who promised to pass my messages on. One Saturday morning I walked over to his house, Mum made me put on a clean shirt, and knocked on the door. Three old women in black, big crosses around their necks were sitting in the lounge. Joe's father, in a bathrobe and boxer shorts, was sipping whisky and watching the cartoons. I greeted him, shifting nervously from one foot to another, and he got up, wrapped his arms around me and covered my face in stoned kisses. Behind him the three old women started a lament, cries of agony, of despair, a chorus of chants that frightened me, and I stiffened in the man's arms: washed in his alcoholic fumes; in the tears falling from his eyes. I remember his bristles biting into my cheeks. Ari, Ari, he murmured, in time to the chants, God has abandoned us. One of the old women pulled me away from him and took me into the kitchen and gave me a glass of coke. She asked after my parents, my brother, my sister, asked how school was going.

–Can I see Joe? I asked. She took me by the hand and we went into the master bedroom. Joe's mother was lying in bed, half-asleep, groaning from time to time, words in Greek that I couldn't understand. Joe was sitting beside her, holding her hand, and Betty, just a child then, was building houses of cards on the floor. She looked up, saw me and winked. Mum's still crazy, Ari, she said with a big smile. Shut up, shut up, the old woman screamed at her and slapped her across the face. The house of cards fell around Betty's feet. I sat next to Joe and looked down at his mother.

Joe's mother looked like a teenager, lying on her wet sheets, falling in and out of sleep, wrapping her hand tight around her son's fingers. I sat with Joe for half-an-hour, we were wordless, listening to Betty's chatter, his mother's groans, the laments of the old women. I avoided Joe's face, looking at the vials of pills on the dresser, watching Betty play cards. Their mother, as they had known her, was dead. That was the reason for the laments. This beautiful young ghost in the bed had taken her place. We remained silent, remembering the dead.

When I got up to leave Joe followed me out and we sat on the verandah, smoking cigarettes, saying nothing much. People would pass the house and ask after his mother. She's fine he would answer, choking on the words, spitting out his hatred. Wogs, he muttered to me, hypocrites. I left him, wanting to go, not wanting to go, and walked home. The shops, the milk bar, the row of cottages I walked past were bathed in the light of a winter's sun. They appeared alien to me that day. I remember walking past them seeing them as if for the first time. That day I began to feel alone in this world. I walked past *Agia Triada*, the Greek church in which I had been baptised in the blood of the holy trinity and I opened the iron door and walked in. I lit a candle and crossed myself, looking for God. No one answered. Of course. I looked at the icon of the Madonna, the picture in a gold frame, and looked past her mysterious smile, noticed the cracks in the purple of her robes, noticed the lipstick marks on the glass. The Madonna was mad. She too must have been beautiful when she roamed the streets of some middle-eastern village claiming that God had deposited his sperm in her belly. I remember thinking this thought, thinking that God would strike me now, that the chandelier hanging from the church ceiling would fall on my head. Nothing stirred in the church. I touched the icon, left the building and outside spat on the church steps. I turned, gathered my fingers into a fist and smashed hard against the iron doors. Fuck you, fuck you, I muttered, going crazy myself, not sure who I was cursing.

Joe returned to school, shaved his head, became a

neighbourhood lout. They locked his mother away for a
while, and his father hit the bottle with a ferocious hunger.
Then the doctors took out what they thought shouldn't be
in his wife's head, pumped her high with drugs and settled
her back into the real world. The father gave up the booze
and the cards and they moved out into the suburbs, to a
neighbourhood where no one knows anybody and whatever
happens in the confines of your four walls is your own
business, your own pain. Joe and I would see each other
every weekend, get stoned, get high together. Over at his
house his mother would make me a drink, give me some
cakes to eat. She moved in her world in slow motion. The
little pills she took kept her safe, her eyes were empty of
colour, of light. Every couple of years Joe's father would
take his wife to Greece, make a trek to a valley where the
Virgin was said to appear. They would drink the holy water,
cross themselves, and still the woman would search through
her bag to get to the little pills that kept her sane. Sanity is
a chemical reaction.

I sit at a table

I sit at a table with my brother, listening in to conversation,
drumming the table in time to the music, reclining back on
the seat. Peter is arguing with Ariadne, who keeps laughing
at him; a deep, warm laugh. She leans close to him so that
he can smell her perfume mingled with her sweat from the
dance. An old man, grey haired and obese, is also arguing
with my brother. Next to him, and across the table from
me, a man with a beard has his arm around a young woman
with round, olive eyes. We have been introduced, quickly,
by my brother but I cannot hold on to their names. A
married couple. The man is involved in the argument. The
woman looks bored, watches the dancing. I look at my
watch. It is past midnight. Soon I should leave. Meet Johnny.

The argument bores me. They are discussing the politics of the Greek community in Melbourne. Words fly around me. My brother is arguing that young people, he points at me, need to be included in the committees and councils. Ariadne disagrees violently, her words coarse and direct. Fuck the Greek community, fuck the Australian community, the Vietnamese, the Italian, the Spanish. She is arguing for a new left, of young people, artists, deviants, troublemakers from all the communities to get together. She wants something new, something radical. This country is so boring, she sighs, I wish I was back in Greece. The men around her disagree. She takes a sip of her drink and gets up to buy another. I have no interest, she tells them, in involving myself with progressive, so-called left-wing Greeks if it is the same faces, the same conservative mob of wogs, married, bourgeois, living in the suburbs, who happen to be able to spout Marx and Lenin. The woman across from me flinches. Ariadne continues: I want to be involved with the deviants, the mad, the creative, all those people that the Greek community despises, that the general Australian community despises. For Christ sake, she screams at them, communism is dead. She walks off.

The conversation continues without her. I tune out and instead watch a fat guy in too tight jeans and a too tight shirt dancing gracefully near our table. His eyes are closed, sweat is dripping down his forehead. He looks ecstatic, as if he's on drugs, but I'm sure it is just the dance.

Ariadne returns and puts a glass of whisky in front of me. Peter, she announces to my brother, I want you to request *Your Two Hands*. I know the song. Peter, arguing politics with the old man, ignores her. I get up, tap her shoulder. I'll do it, I tell her. Upright, anger on her face, staring at my brother, she ignores me for a moment. Then turns, smiles at me and kisses me on the cheek. She winks at me. I go over to the bandstand, motion to one of the guitarists and request the Vamvakaris song for Ariadne. The guitarist knows her and tells me they will play it soon. I go back to the table, sit next to her and whisper in her ear; you have to dance it with me.

-Ari, it would be my pleasure, she answers, turning towards me. I lift my glass and salute her.

-Are you proud of being Greek? she asks. The whole table is looking at me. My brother lights a cigarette and blows the smoke in my direction. The question makes no sense to me. I'm glad I'm Greek, I answer, but I'm not proud of it. I had nothing to do with it. The married woman laughs. That's the most sensible thing I've heard all night, she says to me.

-Are you proud of being Australian? The old man's question feels like an interrogation. The answer is easy. No, no way. Proud of being an Australian? I laugh. What a concept, I continue, what is there to be proud of? The whole table laughs at this and Ariadne gives me a hug. They forget me and continue their conversation. The band finishes a song and the bouzouki begins the sad cry of the Vamvakaris song. I jump up, leap on the dance floor and begin to sway to the music. Ariadne joins me, and we twirl and move around the floor, I mouth the tortured lyrics. *Your two beautiful hands will destroy me.*

Ariadne moves sensuously, coming in close to me, and I drop to my knees before her, clapping my hands together in time with the rhythm, encouraging her in the dance. She motions for me to rise and I leap onto my feet, turn twice on my left foot, twice in the other direction on my right foot. I block the rest of the pub out; do not see the other dancers around me and Ariadne, do not see the band, the crowd. I shut my eyes, Ariadne disappears except for the lingering scent of her sweet perfume, the light trace of tea-tree oil in her hair. I fall and stumble in the hashish rhythms of the song, chasing the agonised cries of the clarinet.

As the words pierce my skull, I see the unshaven face of George appear behind my closed eyelids, morning sun across his face, and I open my eyes. Ariadne is on one knee before me, clapping along to the music, tears of sweat on her brow, her eyes half–closed, singing along to the song. The chorus is repeated for the last time, I fall to my knee in front of her and as the last note is played, held, ends, I lean over her and kiss her tenderly, lightly on the lips. Flirt, she calls me, grabs my hand and leads me back to the table. The band place their instruments down and announce a twenty–minute break. I look at my watch again. Definitely time to go but I keep my grip on Ariadne's hand.

–You're a good dancer, Ari, the married woman tells me.

–What's your favourite song? Ariadne asks me. Hard question. Favourite songs, like favourite films, like favourite people, change day by day, moment by moment. Hard question, I answer.

–What would you like to hear after the break? she insists, not taking a seat. I look over at Peter. Do you think they'd play *What Becomes of the Brokenhearted*? He shakes his head, grins at me, and announces to the table: My brother wishes he was black.

I scowl. I wish no such thing. That the best modern music is black is a simple fact, the logic of the ears, the objective fact of history. My brother, seeing my anger, rises from his seat and begins to hum the Jimmy Ruffin tune. Fired by the dance, fired by the drugs, by the night, I get onto the table and begin to sing the opening verse. Peter gets up, climbs on the table, clicks his fingers in time to my singing and joins in with me at the chorus. *What becomes of the brokenhearted.* Around us, the room has stopped and the crowd is watching us and that spurs me on, my voice louder, competing with the furious buzz of drunken conversations. I lose the tune and collapse into giggles, knock over a glass and jump off the table. Ariadne starts clapping and the people on the tables around us raise their glasses to us.

-Got to go. Ariadne kisses me goodbye. Pleasure to meet you, she tells me. Ditto, I say and head through the crowd, out into the warm summer air. On the way I pass the man in the fishing cap and nod to him. He ignores me. That causes no pain; he was a momentary figure in my life. That's what I like about casual sex with men; there's no responsibility towards the person you fuck with. Outside, sitting on the steps to the pub, Maria is smoking a cigarette and talking to Kosta. Where you going? she asks me.

-To the Punters, I'm meeting up with Johnny.

-Are you clubbing afterwards? Probably going to the Peel, I answer. I kiss her goodbye and head down Glenlyon Road. The lights, the music, the traffic of Sydney Road disappear and I walk down a dark suburban street, whistling the Jimmy Ruffin song. Dogs start barking.

Janet vs Ariadne

Janet vs Ariadne. Janet with her smooth pale skin. Fleshy. Short dyed-red hair. Steel-capped boots and op-shop dresses. Ariadne clothed in silk and expensive shirts and skirts. Luxurious dark hair falling in curls around her face and shoulders. Janet coming over to our house, ill-applied lipstick, chattering away with Mum in English. My father looking at her suspiciously and laying on a thick Greek accent. Alex showed her the family photographs. I took her out back of the shed and shared a joint with her. She told me that I should do my own laundry. I told her that if my mother wanted to slave over her children that was my mother's decision. Dinner was not a success, my father got drunk and abused Australians. Peter got drunk as well, abused my father and abused Greeks.

He took Janet home and returned hours later, waking Mum and Dad up, screaming at them, saying I'm sick of it, sick of living in your world, living in this house, I can't study,

I can't think. I stayed in my room watching the television, watching the American news with the sound turned low so I could hear the screaming. Peter came in my room, tired, pale, his hair plastered across his forehead. Sweating, he had walked all the way back home.

Ari, he whispered to me, taking one of my cigarettes, I'm going to move in with Janet. Sure, I answered, she seems nice. Mum and Dad will make a big fuss, mate, he told me, this might not be a pleasant house for a long time. I got up and turned off the television, sat down next to him. I put my arm around him. It's okay big brother, I can handle Mum and Dad. Peter started crying, a slow, quiet cry. We're not normal wogs are we, Ari? he said quietly. No, thank God for that, I answered.

Families can detonate. Some families are torn apart forever by one small act, one solitary mistake. A marital indiscretion, someone doing drugs, a father fucking a kid up the arse in the bathroom. Living in my family it was a series of small explosions; consistent, passionate, pathetic. Cruel words, crude threats. If we came home late, Mum would wake up and scream that she had given birth to animals, louts, a slut. If we were not doing our homework, Dad would yell at us for being lazy and stupid. Most times you could shrug it off, go to your room, put on music and let them carry on outside.

If they were very angry they might come in, turn off the music, throw your CD or cassette against the wall. The screaming could go on half the night, wake up the neighbours, wake up the dogs. They called us names, abused us, sometimes hit us, short sharp slaps. It was not the words themselves, but the combination of savage emotion and insult, the threat of violence and the taunting tone that shattered our attempts at pretend detachment; it was Peter's sly, superior smile, my sister's half-closed eyes which did not look at them, my bored, blank face, that spurred my parents on to greater insults, furious laments. The words, the insults; spawn of the devil, fucking animals, pieces of shit, the Antichrist, sons of bitches, daughter of a whore, stupid, lazy, ugly, useless, shameful, not–real–men, weak, you embarrass us, we are the laughing stock of the neighbourhood, I regret the day I gave birth to you.

And our replies; peasants, dumbfuck ignorant hillbillies, hypocrites, wogs, dumb cunt wogs. We spurred each other on till we reached a crescendo of pain and we retired exhausted to our rooms, in tears or in fury. Then Peter met Janet and he walked out the door. She offered him a way out. We are weak, lazy, useless, we can't do it on our own, we need the strong back of another. Janet served her purpose, and now Peter's wandering eyes have connected with Ariadne clothed in silk. Beauty is top currency in this world. Not that Janet is ugly, but next to Ariadne she can't compete. And my brother, he's a Greek boy. Thinks with his dick.

Like me. The street is dark and a few blocks south is my brother's house. I could walk down the small inner–city streets, renovated terraces and newly–constructed speed traps, walk across Brunswick Road, past the Italian nursing home and knock on my brother's door. Maybe George would be home, watching television, drinking a beer, we could share a joint. In the darkness I can smell him, the bitter tang of his sweat. But instead I keep walking along Glenlyon Road and go into the Seven Eleven. Bored young Italian boys are hanging out in the car park. They look at me suspiciously, then look away. A young guy behind the counter, pimples on his face, baseball cap on his head, is listening to music on the radio. I buy an orange juice and ask for a packet of cigarettes. Chaka Kahn is on the radio and the young guy turns the volume up. Good song I say to him. He nods and takes my money. I nod and take my change.

Outside, in the car park, Chaka Kahn is also blaring from

a car speaker. I walk towards St George's Road with the fading echo of *Ain't Nobody* falling around my ears.

At St George's Road I stick out my finger and head towards the City. Cars fly past me. I hear occasional shouts and abuse but none of the cars stop. At the lights a young punk girl is vomiting against a wall. Are you okay?, I ask her and she tells me to fuck off. I lean against the lightpost and watch the yellow bile pulse out of her mouth. When she's finished she staggers off across the street, ignoring the traffic and enters a pub. I stay leaning against the post, listening to the acoustic hippie-shit music coming from the pub.

The vomit seeps down the wall and runs in a little stream into the gutter. The wall is plastered with graffiti. Rap art and political graffiti. Act Up is sprayed in red. An anarchy symbol in black. Someone has scribbled Nelson Mandela Was Duped in blue. Underneath, in white, red and blue, a picture of the Madonna. A blank wall on which people want to leave their mark. Like dogs pissing on a shrub. I wish I had a texta on me, to write my name, and then underneath, to write; I'm not saying anything. Instead I keep walking along. A yellow station wagon stops for me and I run and get into the back seat. A red-haired man is driving; beside him sits a woman with long blonde hair. Where are you going? she asks me.

-Just down the road, to the Punters. The man heads off. They don't speak to me, don't speak to each other. Some shit skip band is on the radio. I lean forward and say thanks for the lift. The man grunts. Around my feet are scattered empty hamburger containers from McDonald's, empty cans of coke, wrappers from chocolate bars and cigarette butts. The car smells of dope and french fries. The car stops at the lights and the woman turns around and looks at me. She turns her head slowly, as if her neck can't support the effort required. They are both pinned, and I don't try for any further conversation. They're on heroin, I'm on speed, different drugs, different moods. We are caught up in our separate, individual experiences. Conversation is redundant.

They drop me off at the Punters and Brunswick Street is full of drunks, young suburban couples in their Saturday night best. Across the street a van is playing seventies disco and a tall, thin man is dancing on top of the roof. A sign on the side of the van reads: I have AIDS and I've been fired from work. Please give me some money, I'm dancing as fast as I can. The crowds on the street ignore him except for a group of young anarchists who are trying to make conversation with him. He ignores them, ignores the crowds, his face looking upwards to the night sky, exalted, the sweat pouring like a river around his naked torso. He is spinning on the roof of the van, looking to heaven, finding jubilation in the gospel of disco, music from a time where you could put your dick into anything and not worry about what you would find.

A Maori bouncer stands at the door of the pub. In a blue cap, Malcolm X T-shirt and a red vest, he looks like New York City.

The pub is full of drunken white boys and girls, private school blonde kids doing punk and grunge. Johnny is sitting at the bar, dressed as Toula, talking to a beautiful dark-haired boy in a leather jacket. Johnny is wearing a scarlet, tight mini-dress and black silk stockings. His stilettos are resting against the boy's ankles. Two Ethiopian guys are looking at him suspiciously but Toula has her back to them. The Ethiopian guys are trying to look like Americans; baseball caps, chains and rainbow shirts but they can't pull it off, they don't look comfortable in their clothes. They look like what they are; immigrants just off the boat. I go up to Johnny and stroke his back.

Johnny takes my hand and introduces me to the boy in leather. I have a big grin on my face. The boy's name is Declan and he shakes my hand. Glad to meet you, Ari, he says, but I can't hear the words above the heavy din coming from the band room. I see his mouth move.

I order a whisky from the bar and buy a round of beer for Johnny and Declan. My last shout, I yell to Johnny, I'm running out of cash.

-It's fine, sugar, he tells me, Mama won big at the races today. We're celebrating. Johnny holds out his hand in a tight fist and I take hold of it. He drops two tablets into my palm. I put them in my mouth and take a sip of whisky to wash them down. What have I taken? I ask.

-A cocktail, sugar. The brown one was acid, the white one ecstasy. I told you, Mama won a mint this afternoon. I groan and look at Declan, who laughs at me. I shrug my shoulders and decide to enjoy the night. The little pills are in my stomach now, soon to disintegrate, sliding their magic into my bloodstream and into my brain. A young woman in heavy make-up comes up to Declan and puts her arm around him. She ignores me and Johnny. She whispers something in Declan's ear and he gets up, kisses Johnny on the cheek, shakes my hand goodbye and leaves with the young woman holding onto his arm. I take his seat. That isn't the Croat? I ask. Johnny gives a long laugh. Declan is hardly a Slav name, sugar, is it? He finishes the beer and asks the barman for another.

-No, the Croat left. The night was a disaster. Johnny adjusts his dress. He was angry I was on drugs, he thought I was a nice Greek girl.

-Someone to take home to mother? I ask. Johnny laughs and touches my cheek affectionately.

-Let's go, I'm tired of hanging out in this place. Let's go to the faggots. I finish my drink and take his arm. One of the Ethiopians leans over and whispers something into Johnny's ear. Johnny giggles then whispers something back to the man. The man laughs and waves us goodbye. What was all that about? I ask.

Johnny ignores me and stops to chat with the bouncer. I wait outside, where the man is still dancing on top of the van, the crowds still ignoring him. The anarchists have moved on and are busking further down the street. Disco music from the van mingles with the feedback from the pub, drowning out the acoustic guitars and tambourines of the anarchists. Johnny joins me and looks around for a taxi. What was all that about? I repeat. He wanted to know if you were my boyfriend. Johnny smiles flirtatiously at me, puts on a wog accent. He big cock, he was asking me, boyfriend have big cock?

-What did you tell him? Johnny puts his head back and laughs. He laughs and laughs, drowning out the disco, the grunge band in the pub, the hippies playing guitars.

-I told him that it was big enough but that mine was bigger. He throws me a sly grin. Much bigger. I laugh. It's true. Johnny's hung. A group of drunk skip boys are giving him dirty looks and I put my arm around him, protectively, indicating that I am ready to defend him. The street is too crowded, too well lit for a clash to take place and the drunk boys don't stop us. We cross over to the old post office and wait for a taxi to arrive. Johnny lights a cigarette and immediately a white cab slides across Johnston Street and stops in front of us. I hail it and open the door to the back seat for Johnny. No smoking, the driver warns him. Johnny stands with the door open and slowly smokes his cigarette. I get into the front seat and wait for Johnny to finish his cigarette. What's wrong with your friend? the driver asks me. I look over. He has dark skin, long black hair across his shoulders, wears a blue denim jacket. A young guy, some kind of wog. He has the radio on and the Beach Boys are singing wouldn't it be nice if we were lovers.

-Nothing's wrong with my friend. He's enjoying his cigarette. The driver looks back at Johnny. Get in, he yells, have your fucking smoke but if the cops catch you smoking you pay the fine. Johnny glides in the back. Thanks, sugar, he calls out, settles in the back and the driver asks where we are going. I tell him Collingwood and he hits the steering wheel with his fist. Couldn't you fucking walk? he asks me.

I don't answer, the drugs Johnny has given me must be
starting their effects because I'm sinking into a trance, the
night air is turning to liquid and the sounds in the taxi, the
sounds off the street, are becoming very sharp, very clear. I
can hear a woman's stiletto heels on the pavement, Brian
Wilson's voice isn't coming from the taxi's shit-box radio
but seems to be emerging from inside my head. Johnny
leans forward, flashes the driver a large smile and tells him
to just drive.

   -Just drive, he says, we're large tippers. The driver relaxes
and starts the engine. To Collingwood, he says. To Collingwood, I echo.

Hit the North

Hit the North. The North is where they put most of the
wogs. Not in the beginning. In the beginning we clogged
the inner city and the industrial suburbs of the west. But as
wogs earned some money and decided to move further
afield, into the bush-land-torn-down-to-become-housing-
estates, more and more concrete and brick-veneer palaces
began to be sprinkled across the Northern suburbs. Wogs
were not welcome to move South of the river, the brown
murky Yarra which divides the city, so instead the Greeks
and Italians, the Chinese and the Arabs, began to build their
homes on the flatlands on the wrong side of the river.

   The North, if you're a wog, will entrap you. Push, push,
push against it. Little Arabic communities, little Greek
communities, little Turkish and Italian communities. The
Northern suburbs are full of the smells of goats cheese and
olive oil, hashish and bitter coffee. The Northern suburbs
are unrelentingly flat with ugly little brick boxes where the
labouring and unemployed classes roam circular streets; the
roads to nowhere.

   The North isn't Melbourne, it isn't Australia. It is a little village in the mountains of the Mediterranean transported to the bottom of the southern hemisphere; markets of little old ladies in black screeching in a Babel of languages. Harridans, fishwives, scum. The North is a growing, pulsating sore on the map of my city, the part of the city in which I, my family, my friends are meant to buy a house, grow a garden, shop, watch TV and be buried in. The North is where the wog is supposed to end up. And therefore I hate the North, I view it with as much contempt as possible.

I resist the North, the spaces in which Greeks, Italians, Vietnamese, and the rest of the one hundred and ninety other races of scum, refos and thieves hold on to old ways, old cultures, old rituals which no longer can or should mean anything. I hit the North, get off the bus and walk along the steaming asphalt streets and I want to scream to the fucking peasants on the sidewalk, Hey you, you aren't in Europe, aren't in Asia, aren't in Africa any more. Face it, motherfuckers (and motherfucker is appropriate, the greatest obscenity: the matriarch reigns supreme in these wog houses. She may be kicked and beaten, exploited and hated, but it is she who maintains a rigid grip on the traditions that blighted her life and will blight the lives of her children). Face it motherfuckers, I want to scream, there isn't a home any more. This is the big city, the bright lights of the west, this is a wannabe-America and all the prayers to God or Allah or the Buddha can't save your children now. I put on a scowl and roam the North in my dirtiest clothes, looking and feeling unwashed. I am the wog boy as nightmare.

The reception centres are all in the North, scattered along the suburban shopping strips on High Street and Sydney Road, the centres where weddings, engagements, twenty-firsts are celebrated. We dress up in glittering suits and sparkling dresses to celebrate the timeless rituals of our cultures, dining on second-rate food, listening to second-rate musicians mangle the folk music our parents learned to dance to. Cousins I have not seen in years, aunts who I do not remember, we all sit together and drink toasts to the blushing bride and the handsome groom on the dais and I always feel like choking on my drink, smashing my fist into the wedding cake, sucking off the best man in the toilets, getting drunk, getting ripped, getting out of it, abusing my uncles, doing anything to stop the charade.

In the red glow of the plastic reception centre, the wog is revealed as a conman, a trickster or a self-deluded fool. Thousands of dollars spent recreating the motions of old rituals that have no place or meaning in this city at the bottom of the world. My brother, my sister, myself, my cousins all leave the dinner table, and on the garbage-littered back steps of the reception centre we get stoned, smoke joint after joint, so that we can go back inside, sit at the table, raise a toast without the bile exploding from our mouths. And we sit, red-eyed, almost comatose, looking at the display of wealth before us: a long table piled with boxes of gifts, the table overflowing; money pinned to the bride's dress; balding, fat men throwing notes onto the bandstand; large women, sweating and laughing, jingling their gold bands and bracelets as they move around the circle of the dance. I never dance at weddings.

I hate it, but the North is temptation. I take the bus from the city and roam the ovals and parks and river banks, searching out fat Arab men and chain-smoking Greek men who stand with their dicks out at urinals, cigarette in their mouths, waiting for you. A defiant dance, for I am a wog myself, and I have to force myself to my knees before another wog. I have to force my desire to take precedence over my honour. It is in the North where I search for the body, the smile, the skin that will ease the strain on my groin, that will take away the burning compulsion and terror of my desire. In the North I find myself, find shadows that recall my shadow. I roam the North so I can come face to face with the future that is being prepared for me. On my knees, with hate written on my face, I spit out bile, semen, saliva, phlegm, I spit it all out. I spit on the future that has been prepared for me.

The taxi

The taxi is hovering above the concrete. As if we are flying. We pass the commission flats and I see giant shadows form mutant shapes. Two Cambodian boys are sitting on the lawn eating pizza. I can smell the food. Vegetarian pizza. Mushrooms, capsicum, I roll my tongue along my bottom lip. On the radio the Beach Boys are replaced by Cher. In the back Johnny squeals in excitement and yells at the driver. Turn it up, turn it up. He belts out the song, a deep baritone. The driver turns up the radio and joins in on the chorus. They are singing about turning back time, finding a way to get back with a lover, and I'm laughing. I hate the song but tonight I don't mind the vapid lyrics, the contemptible conventionality of the music.

We are approaching the club but Johnny asks the driver to drive around the block until the song has finished. The driver parks in a side street, turns off the lights and from somewhere underneath his seat he pulls out a joint. More squeals from the back seat. The song ends and the driver turns the radio off. He lights the joint, takes a drag and passes it to Johnny.

–I thought there was no smoking in this cab. The driver doesn't answer the question. You Greek? he asks instead. Sure are. Johnny arches his head forward, obstructing my view of the driver. Just two Greek girls looking for a good night out. I grimace. I don't like Johnny calling me a girl.

–What are you? I ask the driver.

–Turkish. Johnny passes me the joint. Johnny glares at the driver. Your great-grandfather raped my great-grandmother, he threatens him. For a second there is a silence, then the

driver, myself, Johnny begin a ringing of laughter. I pass the
joint back to the man and ask if the customers complain
about the smell. Air freshener in the glovebox, he tells me,
and as he leans across, his face brushes against Johnny's
hair, his hand touches my knee. I shift my leg away, he
opens the glovebox. A clutter of cassettes, cigarettes, I notice
a photo of a fat-faced baby. You like Greek music? he asks.
I have plenty of Greek music.

-Who've you got? I rummage through the cassettes and
pull out a tape of Deep Purple, a Black Sabbath, a Lionel
Ritchie.

-You like Manos Loizos? He picks up an old, battered
tape without a cover. He turns off the radio, puts the cassette
in the deck and hissing fills the taxi. The song *The Road*
comes on. Johnny looks bored. I hate this song, he whinges,
it's so fucking twee. He ignores Johnny and asks me. Do
you like this song?

I like the song. The night outside glistens, the glow from
the street lamps is liquid silk. I mouth the words to the song.
The road has its own story, the story is written by the youth.
I have this song on my favourite tape. I have a specific
memory attached to this song. My father drunk, waving his
hands in the air and dancing. My mother drunk, clapping
along, and Alex, Peter and I watching them, laughing at their
drunkenness, enjoying their joy. My father picks me up and
drags me to the centre of the lounge, pulls me towards him.
In adolescent rebellion I pull away, needing to pull away,
not wanting to. He shrugs, and picks up my mother instead
and dances with her. He does not struggle for my affection.

I ate up the words of the song that night, feasted on their
richness and their promise. His shrug hurt and I consumed
the words to the song and made them mine. I looked at his
body going to fat, inertia chipping away at his dreams, and
the words to the song he was dancing to seemed to be a
challenge, a challenge which he had betrayed, maybe he

had always betrayed, likely he would betray forever. Johnny is right about this song, the music lacks guts, soul even, but the words carry fire and passion. *The road has its own story, the story is written by the youth.* I listen to the song on the Walkman and think that it is better to leave, move away, exit, end the story. Better to leave than stay and become fat and inert.

–I like the song, I reply to the driver. You should like this song, he turns and tells Johnny. This song is about the students gunned down by fascist tanks. You know about the Polytechnic, don't you? His face, in shadow, seems much too large, his teeth much too bright, his eyes are dark and black and I'm panicked for a moment because I can't see any white in his eyes. A demon's eyes. I relax back in the seat. I'm tripping.

  –You Turks are like the Greeks, always on about politics. Johnny turns to me. It's true, Ari, he asks me in Greek, one life and it's all politics, isn't it? One life and it's all politics, the Turk replies in Greek. He sighs and turns the engine on, sprays the cab with air freshener and rolls down his window. Johnny searches through his bag and gives him ten dollars. The driver takes it and doesn't look at him. Johnny taps his shoulder.

  –I do know about the Polytechnic, he tells him.

  –You should care more about it, those people struggled. The driver is insistent, he bangs the wheel with his fist. I open the cab door and say thanks for the joint, thanks for playing the song. You should care, he says one last time. I fumble in my head, trying to think of something nice to say to the man. He's a good guy, shared his joint, we had a laugh. I'm glad they struggled, I tell him. Johnny opens the door and gets out of the cab. He leans through the driver's window and kisses him lightly on the cheek. Thank you, he says, and then adds softly, the Polytechnic is history, you know, happened a long time ago.

-It was not so long ago, he answers and begins to drive off. The sound of Greek music accompanies him. Johnny pulls up his dress and asks me how he looks. Fine, I reply, then noticing his hurt expression, I add, beautiful. He smiles, takes my arm and we walk towards the nightclub, the heavy rhythms of the music inside the disco are shaking the earth; I feel the music vibrate underneath my feet. When was the Polytechnic? Johnny asks me. Sometime in the seventies, I answer, during the junta. Same time as the Vietnam War. Johnny fingers his hair, preparing for his entrance. I was right, he says, it is history.

The Polytechnic is history

The Polytechnic is history. Vietnam is history. Auschwitz is history. Hippies are history. Punks are history. God is history. Hollywood is history. The Soviet Union is history. My parents are history. My friend Joe is becoming history. I will become history. This fucking shithole planet will become history. Take more drugs.

The crowd at the door

The crowd at the door is impatient, much lighting of cigarettes, much shuffling of feet. Johnny and I go to the front of the queue. The bouncer, his black T-shirt pulled tight across his chest, waves us inside. On our way in he pats Johnny on the arse. Once inside my eyes, ears, my skin is assaulted by sensation. The drugs are making me fly. A thick crowd of men surrounds the bar and each of them looks up, surveys me, Johnny, then each one returns to his drink or to his solitary search for a fuck. The music belts me across the face and I cannot decipher a tune, a melody, a rhythm. Bass dominates the club. Johnny lets go of my hand and wanders to the bar. I follow him and plant myself beside him, lean on the bar, look at the world around me.

Two blond boys in white T-shirts and jeans repeat the same motions behind the bar. They ask for the order, take the money, prepare the drink, hit the till, serve the drink to the customer, hand over the change. Johnny waits to be served. At one end of the bar, close to the cigarette machine, a man keeps shyly looking towards me. I pull my gaze away from his but I find my eyes returning to search for him. I'm seeking an assurance that he finds me sufficiently attractive, so attractive that he will risk my dismissal of him, that he is prepared for my turning away from him. I cannot define his appearance, his age, his style; he is blending into the vibrant mutating mass of the club. He lifts a glass towards me. I nod then turn away and begin talking to Johnny.

–What will you have to drink? he asks me. I ask for a whisky and Johnny yells the order to the barman. The barman smiles at me and I notice, beneath the glare of the bar lights, that his blond hair is thin, that he is balding. We get the drinks and sit at the bar. Johnny wraps an arm around me and whispers in my ear. You tripping yet, sugar? Sure, I reply, I'm tripping man. A group of women in black leather enter the club and the men look at them suspiciously. One of the women, a young girl in a leather bra and tight black shorts, her hair cropped close to the skull, gelled, comes up and gives Johnny a hug. She kisses me and I smell coconut oil in her hair, sweet perfume on her neck. Sasha adjusts her leather bra and asks how we are. Out of our fucking skulls sugar, Johnny replies, and gives her a sip of his drink.

–You still with Georgie? I ask. Sasha ignores the question and talks to Johnny.

–Toula, you got any speed, know anywhere to get some? I want to party and the fucking dykes I'm with aren't in the mood. She winks and points to one of the women. A tall, pale, beautiful woman, the leather wrapped tight around her

large, muscled frame. Except for her, Sasha winks again. I
think I can party with her.

   -I guess you're not still with Georgie. Sasha doesn't hear.

   -I don't do speed, sugar, you know that. Only bliss drugs
and I'm all out. The beautiful Ari took my last tab. Johnny
touches me softly under my chin. His touch makes my skin
pulsate. I look around the crowd, turn back to see the man
at the end of the bar, still looking at me. What do you say,
Ari, Johnny asks me, can you help this sweet young girl in
distress?

   -Sweet my arse, Sasha says, and she turns to me. Have
you got something, Ari? I shake my head but tell her I'll
scout and see if I can find anything. She blows me a kiss,
takes my hand and slips me a fifty-dollar note. I get up from
the bar and ask them to wait for me. I begin to wander
around the labyrinth of the club.

   At the edge of the dance floor a line of men watch the
gymnastics of the dancers. The fast furious dance music
propels me closer to the first circle of dancers and I watch
mesmerised as a young short dancer weaves his elastic hips
to the music. Drugs mould the club, drugs initiate the
dancing, the search for sex. The smell of amyl, the boys
with clenched jaws on speed, the girl in the middle of the
dance floor waving her long arms towards the disco ball,
lost in an acid dream, the alcohol that lubricates our
movements around each other, the joints rolled in dark
corners. Without the drugs the music would be numbing,
monotonous. Without the drugs the faces would be less
attractive; wrinkles, bad teeth, double chins. I sniff the smell
of marijuana and I'm happy.

   I leave the edges of the dancing and move to the back
of the club. Faces stare at me and I ignore them, content to
be an object of admiration, feeling a surge of power. A hand
brushes across my crotch and I glare at the man who touches
me. He offers a short, insipid laugh. I want to smash his face
in but I move on, searching for a connection, wanting to

find some drugs for Sasha so she will admire me. Her beauty is tantalising; her admiration I would treasure. A young boy wearing a football beanie and an Indian cotton jacket is sitting cross-legged on a table. I walk up, offer him my hand and he takes it, punches me lightly on the shoulder and asks how I am.

–Cool, I reply, doing fine. Rat is beautiful, handsome, child of a wild, hard-drinking Italian whore. His father was a Maori who Rat has never met; two more adult fuckups but their brief union produced a glorious boy whom I always ache to touch. But we hesitate in our physical communions. Testing each other, not wanting to be the first to admit desire. The first to be the faggot.

–I'm looking for quick, Rat, got any? He nods and I sit beside him on the table. Look at that queen, he says, pointing to a bald old man in a tuxedo, sweating from the manic dancing. He begins to drum his fists on the table. I hate this fucking music, he tells me. It's shit.

–That queen with the Dali moustache is DJ tonight, he continues. Go up and request something, he'll play it for you. He snickers. He likes you, likes the Greek boys. I laugh and put my arm around Rat. He lifts his arm, takes my hand and I slip him the money. What do you want to hear? I ask him. I'll request something for you but the prick probably won't play it.

–Ask for some rap, acid-metal, hardcore techno. Anything with fucking guts. Rat spits out the words. I'm tired of this faggoty high-energy shit. He leans over and whispers to me, the shit is in my jacket pocket. I put my hand in the pocket closest to me and I touch the warm sleeping body of a large mouse. Dewey, Rat's pet, is taken everywhere. I put my arm around him again and search his other pocket. My fingers touch a plastic packet and I pull it out the pocket and slip it into my jeans. Thanks mate, I say and get up to leave.

–I'll request something for you but they aren't going to play any hardcore nigger shit here. Just pansy nigger shit.

Rat smiles and punches me lightly again on the shoulder. Black and proud, he says. I walk away, and he yells after me: Sister Sledge, *Lost in Music.* I give him the thumbs up and walk through the dancers, brushing against bodies, pushing myself against young Asian boys lost in a frenzy of dancing; singing along to the trite pop lyrics. I throw my head back and give off a number of loud screams. Add my voice to the music.

The door to the DJ's booth is closed but I open it and walk in. A middle-aged lesbian is smoking a joint and frowns at me. Get out, she warns. It's alright, I say to her, I know him. The DJ winks at me and the woman relaxes and offers me the joint. The DJ is mixing in a new song and ignores me for a moment. I sit back and enjoy the cocoon of peace inside the booth. He finishes, takes off the headphones and sits down with us, taking the joint.

–What you want? he asks. Thrash, rap, something loud I ask him. He shakes his head. Not on a Saturday night, Ari, he tells me, the queens are not going to get off on that straight shit. The woman starts to argue with him.

–Why is it straight? She points at me. This wog here is right, play something tough you fucking old poof. The DJ ignores her and asks me if I want to hear anything else.

–*Lost in Music.* Sure, he shrugs, we'll play that. But later, stick around. Fine, I say, and get up, thanking the dyke for the joint. And play *Temptation* if you've got it. Heaven 17. He nods again. Sure, later.

Every time I look

Every time I look at a gay man, even if I think he's attractive, I can't forget he's a faggot. I get off on real men, masculinity is what causes my cock to get hard, makes me feel the sweet frenzy and danger of sex. No matter how many hours spent at the gym, no matter the clothes he wears, the way he cuts his hair, the way he talks, a gay man always reveals himself as a faggot. I'm not talking about queens. Queens are cool. Bitchy but cool. They are not hung up on being a man, they are quite happy to act like schoolgirls. I don't sleep with queens. They don't do anything for me.

I sleep with faggots but they always disappoint me. The desperate effort to hide his effeminacy always betrays him. I can see it in myself. But I do a good job of talking-like, walking-like, being a man. I've got the build, the swagger, the look. More, I've got the fuck-ya-I-don't-give-a-shit attitude perfected to an art form. Faggots love sleeping with me, they think they've scored a real man. Being a wog is a plus as well. I hate the Greek macho shit, I hate the Latin macho shit, I hate the macho shit, period, but the truth is that the faggot scene is a meat market and the tougher the meat the bigger the sale. It's vanity, I know it's nothing more, but I get a buzz out of faggots thinking I'm straight. The pleasure is not all mine. The faggot sucking on my cock is getting a thrill as well, he is thinking to himself; I've scored myself a one hundred percent genuine wog boy.

But mostly I come to gay bars to dance. For the real sex that gets me off, the sex that makes me shudder in ecstasy, I do the beats. That's where I find my real men.

I got it

I got it. I tap my pocket. I got the speed. Sasha throws her arms around me and I touch her lithe, her so thin body. She's skin and bone but still she feels softer than a man. Johnny applauds me. We're proud of Ari, he tells Sasha, he can draw the men and the drugs. Johnny winks at me and I slip my arms off Sasha, put my hands in my pocket and smile. One hundred percent Greek stud. Sasha introduces me to the woman she likes, her name is Angie. A drag joins our circle, a tall black man with a blonde wig. He throws his

arms around Johnny and screams in a loud American accent;
Toula, Toula you bitch, where have you been? I turn away
from the squeals and order another whisky from the bar.
The barman, looking exhausted, flashes me a weak smile.
Bad night, mate? I ask.

-Fucking awful. He pours a double serve of alcohol for
me and offers me the drink with a wink. Is she your girlfriend? he asks, pointing at Johnny. Johnny, still exchanging
conversation with the drag, hears and turns around. He
waves a finger at the barman. We're family, sugar. And
anyway, Ari here, he only has real men, don't you? The
drag stops his conversation and stares at me. He runs his
tongue over his bottom lip. My boyfriend's Greek, he tells
me, you Greeks love the black girls, don't you? I don't
answer, give the barman some money and take a sip of my
drink. Should we have some of the speed? I ask Sasha, and
she nods and takes Angie's hand. See you later, I say to
Johnny. The drag moves aside to let me pass and I kiss
him lightly on the cheek. He runs a hand down the front
of my T-shirt and tells me his name is Crystal. He whispers
it in my ear and I shiver as his warm breath hits my
eardrum. I don't move away till he's close to touching my
balls. Then I leave and follow Sasha and Angie into the
women's toilets.

The three of us crowd into a cubicle and I squat and
wipe the black toilet lid with paper and pour half the speed.
Let's have it all, Angie says, but Sasha wants a quarter for
afterwards. I pour out a little more. While I cut it up, the
two women start kissing. Angie is pressing Sasha against the
door and moving her hands into Sasha's tight shorts. I snort
a line and leave them two big lines each. Sasha has her go
first, taking small snorts and Angie rests her hand on my
shoulder. So, what are you, she asks, gay, straight or bi? Sasha
looks up. This hurts, she complains, rubbing her nose. Angie
starts rubbing my crotch and I get a hard-on. She stops and
crouches next to Sasha and snorts the speed vociferously.

Two short intakes of air, one in each nostril, and the speed is gone. She stands up and faces me. Her tone is aggressive. So what are you, Ari, she asks again, gay, straight or bi? Sasha gets up and grabs my hand. A slut aren't you, Ari, she says.

-A slut, I agree. Let's go, Sasha says, let's dance. I'll join you in a minute I tell them, and Sasha kisses me on the mouth and says thanks for the speed. Pleasure, I answer. They walk out, holding hands, and Angie pinches me hard on the balls. Too hard, it hurts. Pleasure, she mimics and they close the cubicle door behind them.

I sit on the toilet seat, hang my head low, and sweat gathers on my brow. The toilet seems to shake along to the music. I close my eyes and a red light appears inside my head. A shifting, quivering ray of scarlet which draws me into its trail. I open my eyes and the red light is still there, in front of me. I move my hands towards it and it disintegrates into a shattering of minute crystals. Fucking hell, man, I groan to myself, you're tripping. I get up, take a piss, splashing a spray of urine onto the toilet floor. The smell is pungent. I'm slightly nauseous. I take a deep breath and the nausea leaves, to be replaced by a sensation of joy which starts at my gut and envelops my body. The sound of the music from the club crashes into the cubicle and a soulful woman's voice rides the patterns of the drum machine. Her voice, her delight in making music, making noise connects with the pleasure emanating from my gut and I flush the toilet, and rush out onto the dance floor.

The sea of dancers are jubilant. I run straight into the middle of the crowd and throw my head back and begin to dance, jumping, swaying, following the patterns of the singer's voice. I slide up close to Angie and Sasha who are rubbing their crotches together and we dance in a small circle. The LSD, the ecstasy, the speed, the dope, the alcohol rush around my body and I feel one with the pulsating crowd. Underneath the song a new track forms, and I hear Nile

Rogers' guitar. I yell loudly and punch the air with my fist
as *Lost in Music* thunders out of the speakers and drenches
the club with its thundering hot current.

A tap on my shoulder and Rat is in front of me, his head
hung low, dancing intently. I move close to him, and he
takes out a bottle of amyl from his pocket and takes a sniff.
He passes it to me, I inhale some and pass it on to Sasha.
The fumes eat into my brain and I feel the sweet joy of
chemical death; I fix my eyes on the image of Jimi Hendrix
on Rat's T-shirt. My mouth is moving, I feel it moving, and
I'm singing along to the song, as are the other dancers in
the club. We're lost in music. The song takes me higher and
higher, the crescendo of bass beats lifts me into the
stratosphere. I turn away from the Hendrix T-shirt and
confront a quartet of Filipino boys who are dancing. They
move along to the music in small, elegant little dance steps,
not throwing themselves into the dance as is the crowd
around them. One of them notices me looking and looks
down, giggling. I turn away and am enmeshed in the music
again. The song tails off to be replaced by a thudding high-
energy beat and I weave away from the dance floor. The
Filipino boy smiles at me and I ignore him. His slim body
does not attract me.

My throat is dry and I head back to the bar. I rest my
head on Johnny's shoulder and ask him if he could buy me
a drink. He's still talking to Crystal and they've drawn a
crowd around them. Johnny strokes my chin and buys me
a drink. Too much dancing, sugar.

–Too much speed, I mutter and I pour the whisky down
my dry throat. The barman has gone, replaced by an older
man with a moustache. Crystal puts his arm around my
shoulder and shakes his head at me. Speed is a dirty drug,
he tells me. So is alcohol, I reply and finish off the whisky.

–Maybe I should take you home, Johnny says.

–That sounds like fun, Crystal giggles. A high, feminine
squeal. I turn away from him and order another drink. I hear

Crystal giggle again. He's anyone's tonight, I hear him say to Johnny. Not yours, you fucking Yank bitch. I don't say the words. They explode in my head. The barman slams the drink down in front of me and asks if we are going to crowd the bar all night. I take the drink.

A thin, tall man with long hair in curls comes up to us and grabs Crystal from behind. He bites his ear softly. Crystal thrusts his arse against the man's groin and introduces him to the rest of us.

–This is Con, Costa really. Crystal giggles again. My Greek boyfriend, he adds putting on a wog accent. Con is dressed in a dirty black bomber jacket, faded jeans and cheap, department store runners. His pupils are tiny little holes. Crystal's sweet Greek boyfriend is another junkie wog. He keeps kissing Crystal on the ears, on the neck, but keeps looking up, straight at me. I take slow sips from the glass, not saying anything. Con and me let the drags do most of the talking.

I'm introduced to him and I shake his hand firmly. He calls me mate. Johnny is introduced as Toula. Con starts laughing at the name. Not a very original name, he says. Johnny scowls. That was my mother's name, he says.

–Apologise to Toula, Crystal tells his boyfriend. Con says sorry in Greek, but he still has a smirk on his face. I have a smile on my face as well. Toula is a stupid name. Johnny notices my smile and turns around to Con again. Maybe you'd prefer Ari's stage name, he says. My stomach becomes a tight fist. Shut the fuck up, Johnny. But Johnny ignores me. We call him Persephone. You know the story don't you, she spends half her time in hell, the other half in the real world. Johnny glares at me. Tonight our sweet little Persephone is slumming it in hell. Crystal starts giggling again. I want to smash his pockmarked painted face in. Johnny puts an arm around me and I pull it off violently. He ignores me and keeps talking. The trouble is our little Persephone is beginning to enjoy her time in hell. Aren't you, sugar?

You don't know what's real any more, do you?

-Fuck off, Johnny. I start to walk away. Fuck off you cunt, I yell at him. Crystal starts giggling but Con tells her to shut up. He doesn't look at me either. Fuck off Johnny, I yell, and walk into the crowd.

-It's Toula, he yells after me, it's Toula, sugar. Johnny's not here tonight. It's the girls night out tonight. I don't answer. I walk towards the video games, brushing past people and glaring at the men looking at me. Fuck you, Johnny, I mutter under my breath, I'm no girl. I murmur the words softly so the men around me won't hear.

Johnny is Johnny

Johnny is Johnny to me, he can be Toula to everybody else. I put some coins in the machine and start playing Galaga, shooting away at the little spaceships, the trip intensifying my concentration. I'm scoring high. Johnny and I became friends playing Galaga after school, player one and player two. In dirty coffee shops with old Greek men playing cards on stained tables. Johnny shooting better than me, better than Joe, telling us dirty jokes his father had passed on to him. I shoot spaceships and think of Johnny. Smoking joints under a poster of Molly Ringwald, listening to the soundtrack of *Pretty in Pink*. Getting drunk with his father, listening to the old man abuse his son, Johnny holding my hand under the table.

The game is over and my anger towards Johnny subsides. Johnny's mother died when he was a young child. He carries her photo around with him all the time, a photo of a young, scared woman. A black and white photo of a young girl just having landed on foreign soil which she was to detest and in which she was to be buried. Johnny grew up with an alcoholic father who had no idea of how to look after a child, who gave him over to aunts and neighbourhood women to raise, women who had their own kids and their own husbands and their own work and houses to look after.

Johnny grew up into a shy boy, happiest watching old black and white movies on television, playing video games at arcades. He dragged me off to revivals of Bette Davis movies, I went with him to *Pretty in Pink* four times so he could wallow in Molly's presence. The fourth time he turned to me at the end of the movie, grabbed my hand and told me he wanted to be just like Molly. Except I would have gone with Duckie, he told me, I would have ditched that wimp Andrew McCarthy. I didn't answer, I had figured out that my friend was a faggot. I couldn't answer. I was trying to figure out what I was myself, attacked at night by dreams and fantasies which disturbed me. Spurting out semen in bucketloads, wanking in toilet blocks in Richmond, in Collingwood, in East Melbourne. I never said anything to Johnny. I kept the nightmares to myself but Johnny knew, he smelt the come on me, smelt where my desires were taking me.

Johnny taught me about movies. We watched *A Streetcar Named Desire*, eating chips, drinking ouzo, under his bedsheets, getting erections over Marlon Brando. Of course we fucked. We fucked each other, and we sucked each other, and we wanked each other. We were two horny Greek boys under the bedsheets together. Of course we fucked.

Johnny taught me about music. While our friends and cousins were listening to heavy metal and the top forty, Johnny would scrounge op-shops in Smith Street and Greville Street searching for old disco twelve-inches. He and my brother Peter would make compilation tapes for me, mixing in punk, rap, house, old funk, new funk. Johnny gave me attitude, a sense of style, an arrogance to take on the world. We wagged school often. I had Johnny, I didn't need history, geography, mathematics. I didn't want to learn how to be a conscientious clerk, an effective part of the assembly line. I didn't want to be a good lawyer, a good doctor, a good accountant. How many accountants does the fucking Greek community need? Johnny would yell at his father. What do you want to be, what the fuck are you going to become? you lousy poofter, his father would scream back at him. A movie star, Johnny would answer, smiling at me. I wouldn't answer. I'd sneak another ouzo from his father's bottle.

Johnny dropped out of school early, first chance he got. We got drunk together at the back of the high school, celebrating his decision, throwing our beer cans into the river. He told me that his father had started sleeping with him, getting drunk, coming home smelling of cheap spirits and getting into bed with Johnny. I listened and said nothing. Johnny didn't go into details, he just wanted to tell someone. We got very drunk that night and smashed a few windows of the school. I'm fucking out of here, fucking out of here, Johnny screamed into the night air. I gave him a round of applause and took Johnny home. His father had fallen asleep, drunk in his own bed. That night I went home to bed and masturbated thinking of my best friend's father fucking my best friend.

The night I received my final year results Johnny came and dragged me away from my parents who were screaming abuse. So he failed, Johnny told them, you've got one son at university already. How many do you want there? My father started screaming at him as well. We left the house and he told me he had a surprise for me. We went back to his house and he lit me a joint and left me sitting on his bed flicking through movie magazines. He went off into the bathroom and emerged, twenty minutes later, in a red dress, thick make-up, his hair up in a bun, looking like a woman in a black and white photograph, a scared young woman on foreign soil. What do you think? he asked me. I groaned. Johnny, Johnny that's too much.

–I'm disappointed in you, Ari, he retorted. Never, ever, ever think anything is too much. He sat beside me on the bed. This life is shit, man, uncompromising. He put his arm around my shoulder and I smelt perfume. Haven't we always said, he continued, that what we hate about the wogs is that they are gutless? They don't take chances, don't upset the status quo. He fiddled with a strand of long black hair. Well, Ari, it's not just the wogs. It's all of them. I'm not scared, he shouted defiantly in Greek. Maybe so his old man could hear. I remained silent.

–Don't die on me, Ari, he implored me, don't become like the others. I took his hand and led him out to the lounge room and his father stood up and started yelling at him. Johnny ignored him and I tried to hide in a corner. His father grabbed the bottle he was drinking from and rushed towards his son. Yianni, he screamed, you go out like that, you go out like that you slut, and I promise you, Yianni, I'll fucking kill you. Johnny didn't flinch, didn't make a sound as the bottle smashed on the wall next to him. I'm not Yianni, he told his father, slowly, deliberately, Toula is back. He spat at his father. Toula is back from the grave, papa. He called out to me. Ari, let's go, we've got some celebrating to do. I waved goodbye to Johnny's father, wanting to say something to wipe away the man's shame, staying silent because there was nothing I could say; and walked out into the twilight, Johnny on my arm.

Five transcendental moments

Five transcendental moments in my life, five moments in which my desire, my sexuality, my dreams were not clouded by confusion, ambiguity and regret. By which I learned the five commandments of freedom.

One. Walking out of the house with Johnny, dressed as Toula, walking past the stares and whispers of the neighbours. Thou shalt not give a shit what people think.

Two. My father screaming at me, you failure, you animal,

and my soaking in the contempt, suffocating in my guilt. Then watching my mother throw the same words, the same expressions to my brother as he is walking out of the house. Seeing him drenched in the stench of her venom. Not believing them for my brother. Not believing them for my sister. A glimpse, a slither of light in the darkness of the Greek family drama. Thou art not responsible for thy parents' failure.

Three. Watching Marlon Brando take off his T-shirt in *A Streetcar Named Desire*, a young kid watching the tiny image on a black and white screen. A young kid bursting with semen and sex. My first conscious desire for another man, a man I would like to grow up and become. Thou can have a man and be a man.

Four. The accumulated media crap in my head. The endless list of atrocity, so persistent, so constant that evil becomes banal. The four men of the Apocalypse riding on, again and again and again, through the TV set at six sharp every night. I grew up with these images, thought I had become immune to these images until one night I watched a community service ad sponsored by McDonald's, in which a Somalian woman placed her hand in boiling water, then ripped off the burnt skin from her arm to feed her dying child. At the end of the ad a journalist on behalf of McDonald's asked us to dig into our pockets in order that women like this may live. Thou shalt despise all humanity, regardless of race, creed or religion.

Five. An old man, effeminate and frail, fearfully offers me fifty dollars if I let him suck my cock. I let him do it for free. Next night I go to my first gay bar and pick up a handsome young guy with a good car and a good job. I only agree to fuck him if he gives me fifty bucks. He argues, but can't resist me. I'm sixteen. Thou shalt never steal from the poor or the old but fuck the rich for all it's worth.

Transcendence is the acceptance of the original sin. Realising that to be born human is to be born fucked up.

Transcendence is realising that people do not deserve pity or love or compassion. People deserve contempt. Or, as Johnny says, I may see no future but I got ethics.

A twirling ship

A twirling ship comes for me and I try to hide in the left-hand corner. The shower of missiles, however, attack my ship and the screen flashes Game Over.

Con comes up and passes me a drink. He sits on top of a pinball machine and takes out a cigarette. He offers me one and I take it, light it and lean against the machine. He adjusts his position so his leg is resting against my side. I don't move away. His foot taps along to the exaltations of the disco chanteuse. Drags, they're bitches aren't they? he says. Waits for my answer.

–Sometimes. I take a puff of smoke in my lungs.

–She's not your girlfriend, is she? he asks pointing across to the bar.

–Who Johnny? No he's just a friend. My mouth is still dry, and I take a large sip. The blouse on the woman opposite is moving, small waves running up and down her back. Silk material which catches the flashing lights and sends moonbeams straight into my eyes. I force my eyes away to stop the hallucinations. Con is smiling at me. I never met a wog drag before. He drinks from his beer. Her folks don't know, do they?

–Sure, his old man does. I'm pissed off he keeps calling Johnny a she. His mother is dead.

–Sorry, I didn't know. It's probably for the best. I look at him, not understanding his response.

–I mean, he continues in Greek, if she wasn't dead seeing her son in a skirt would have finished her off. Con begins to giggle. I can't help it, I find myself giggling as well. His whole body is shaking and he puts his hand on my shoulder to steady himself on the machine. He doesn't remove his hand, and I let it stay on me. Do your folks know? he asks me.

-Know what? I reply sharply. The hallucinations don't stop. Con's face is large, imposing, the bristles on his cheeks are making waves. My folks know shit about what I do, I answer, it's better that way.

-Sure is. He gets off the pinball machine and leans over to me, his mouth whispering words close to my ear. A streak of saliva hits my earlobe and I get a hard-on. You're a good-looking guy, Ari, he tells me and runs a hand over my thigh, across my crotch. He strokes my dick and laughs. Seems you think I'm a good-looking guy as well. I try to keep a straight face. The drugs, however, are making me giggle. An older man in a yellow top walks past us and stops to look at us. Con gives a disgusted groan. Fuck off old man, he says loudly, the words lost in the sounds of the arcade games. The man doesn't hear. He keeps looking at us.

-I want to fuck you. Con whispers the words hard against my ear. I'm drifting, I'm adrift on a chemical sea and the words take some time to connect with my brain. His hand is still stroking my cock, the older man watches us. My breathing is creating sonic commotion inside my head. Con is looking at me, waiting for an answer.

-No one fucks me. Con laughs. Sure, Ari, he says, moving his hands away from me. I didn't figure you for a girl. He says the word in Greek, *koritsaki*, a little girl. It sounds like he's laughing at me. Can I fuck you? I ask. Con stops laughing. For a moment, I think he's going to bash me. But he doesn't, instead he puts an arm around me and points a long middle finger to the man looking at us. Fuck off pervert, he yells loudly. The man blushes, throws us a dirty look and walks away. Other people hear us, they look up, murmur to each other, then look away. I catch sight of Con and me, reflected in the black screen of a video game, two dark boys, handsome, strong. We look good. Can I fuck you? I repeat.

The club is now crammed tight with people, mostly men. The music is a savage ceremony, men walking around each other, making eye contact, flirting, but flirting in a detached, cynical manner, to avoid the humiliation of rejection. The women are mostly on the dance floor, thrusting their hips to one another, oblivious to the games of male sexual conquest around them. A few very drunken men, or out-of-it men are putting on an aggressive manner and asking for sex from strangers, loudly and insistently.

It is nearing three o'clock and the club is drenched in sweat and amyl. The whole atmosphere is making me want to puke, I can't create a space to separate me from the other bodies milling around me and Con. I place a hand on the pinball machine, to steady myself. As from a distance I hear Con say something to me. Come on, his words make contact with me. Come on, he starts walking away, let's get out of here.

We walk past the bar and Johnny and Crystal look at us and I avoid their eyes. Past the bouncers and we are in the night air. A hot-dog vendor is selling hot dogs to some leather men. He looks stoned, bored and doesn't respond to the good-natured flirting. Taxis abound on the street, and the drivers have formed a small circle across the street from the club, big men with beer guts, slagging off the queens. Con walks in front of me and I follow him down an alley at the side of the club. Two young blond men are sharing a joint and we walk past them. Have a good time one of them calls out in a high falsetto.

At the end of the alley Con scales a brick wall and I leap up after him. The night is warm. We are in an abandoned factory yard, bricks, high grass and broken glass around our feet. Con looks around then he is on top of me, pushing me back against the wall and kissing me hard on the mouth. I kiss him back and he drags down the zip of my pants and grabs my cock. He kisses me. On the mouth. On the neck. On my chest. He pulls his dick out and thrusts it against my balls. Suck me, I order, and he gets on his knees.

Shadows move and mutate across the walls of the derelict building.

–Suck me. I thrust my cock deep into Con's throat and he pulls away. I grab the back of his head and force his throat back onto my cock.

I look up to the night sky and a star bursts.

–Don't come. Con is back on his feet, both of us with our pants around our ankles. He thrusts against me and has a small brown bottle in his hand. He takes a sniff and passes it to me.

–I want you to fuck me. He whispers the words into my ears and the amyl takes effect. I eat his mouth, grab as much of his flesh as I can in my hands, lick my palms and knead the head of his cock with my fingers. He groans. Every breath he takes envelops my body, makes my flesh burn. I run a hand across his arse. It is taut and hairy. The rush of the amyl subsides.

–Okay. Let me fuck you. I turn him around and take a condom out of my wallet, slip it on my dick, spit into my hands and rub the saliva over the rubber. I push hard against his arse, find the hole and try to push in. He is tight and I can't enter. I lean back.

–Lick my fingers. He sucks on my fingers, then I push them into his arsehole. His head is leaning against the wall. A spider sits placidly inside a hole in the mortar. Above my head more stars are bursting. I kiss the back of Con's neck and push my cock into his arsehole again. This time I'm in and I start a hurried, frenzied fucking.

–It hurts. A whisper through clenched teeth. I ignore him. He groans again, bends completely over and searches the ground for a bottle of amyl. He sniffs and his cock starts to get hard again. He passes the bottle to me.

–Fuck me, wog. He groans.

The spider sits placidly.

My thrusts are getting faster.

Above me the stars are no longer bursting, instead some of them emit long rays to one another, a silver cobweb in the sky.

My thrusts are getting faster.

Con's cock feels huge in my hand.

I thrust hard into Con's arse.

–Oh God, this hurts. His pain excites me and I throw all of myself violently into his arsehole. I look up. The cobweb disintegrates in the sky, an explosion of silver light. I burst inside of Con and fall, slumped onto his body.

I pull out. The wet condom hangs loosely on the tip of my still erect dick, wet, full of my white semen. I dump it on the ground and Con stands up tall and forces me on my knees. His cock rubs against my lips and I take it in my mouth.

Con takes more amyl.

–Suck it, wog. His body is sweating. I close my eyes and concentrate on not throwing up. A deep thrust. A sudden stream of liquid. I drink it in. I don't spit it out, I keep his cock in my mouth drinking in all the sperm he is emitting. I think; is he clean? I stop thinking. Drink in the last of his come and he is groaning. He falls to his knees, sits beside me. I look up. No spider, no fireworks in the sky. We are two boys, sitting on tall grass and broken glass, our pants around at our feet. Our wet dicks fall limp across our sweaty legs.

Con takes out a hanky, wipes himself and passes it to me. He pulls up his pants and takes a cigarette from his pocket. He hands it to me, lights it, then lights one for himself. I am silent, slightly sullen. I'm no good at conversation after a fuck. I suck gladly on the cigarette. It clears the taste of come still on my tongue.

Con gets up, cigarette hanging from his lips and pisses against the wall. He takes a long time to get a stream going. Junkie.

–You clean, aren't you, Ari? I nod. I don't bother to ask

him the same question. He answers it for me, anyway.

 –I'm clean. You're one of the few people I've ever let fuck me. He sits beside me again. It's because you're a man, he adds. I look over at him. He no longer seems quite the masculine Greek man I met a short while ago. His voice sounds an octave higher, he is waving his arms around. Fucking him has feminised him in mind. It could be the drugs. I hold out the handkerchief. You want this?

Throw it away. Save Mum from having to wash up my dirty work. He leans over and kisses me on the mouth. My desire has gone. I close my eyes, think of George and kiss him back. He's not George. I pull away. You going to tell Crystal? I ask him.

 –Shit no. He throws me a puzzled look. What business is it of hers?

I stand up and take a piss. A long stream of urine, pissing out alcohol, water, amyl, marijuana, speed, LSD, ecstasy. Fuck, I groan, I'm drug-fucked. Con gets up as well and starts scaling the fence. I'll buy you a drink he calls down to me. Sure, I answer, I'll have a scotch. We jump the wall and head back to the loud music, to the cruising crowd. The sex we have just had is already disappearing from my mind.

I became a slut

I became a slut. It just happened. First time, the first time remains crystal clear. A middle-aged guy in a tracksuit blowing me in the bushes at Burnley Oval after school. The first time with a girl, a bedroom at some party. Getting off on licking her breasts, she wouldn't let me fuck her, coming on her stomach. A parade of men in toilets, cousins of friends or friends of girls at school. Getting fucked once by a good-looking Turk with a big cock. Hating it, it hurt. Not using a condom and going into an anonymous surgery to do tests. Finding out the results, feeling like I received a second chance and going straight down to a toilet block and getting sucked off.

Fucking Betty, a condom splitting and worried about her getting pregnant. On the phone every day, hoping to hear the magic word: period.

Going to clubs, straight clubs, gay clubs, mixed clubs, grunge clubs, wog clubs, skip clubs, black clubs. Asian boys. Contemptuous Greek and Arab boys. Scared Greek girls, wanting you to bugger them so they can maintain their virginity. Stoned Anglo girls, their cunts smelling of fruity perfume.

Fucking in bedrooms, toilets, cars, under railway bridges, on the beach, in strange lounge rooms, in the back row of porn cinemas. Coming home, late from school, Mama asks Where you been? You answer, out with friends. Having a shower to get rid of the smell of perfume, of aftershave. Getting rid of the smells that linger from a five-minute thrashing of bodies.

Fucking, not falling in love. I'm not much for conversation. Even with girls (and it's easier to converse with girls) I don't seem to have much to say. The more they talk the more you realise you are not the same. Sometimes, it happens, you are in the middle of a fuck–looking into the eyes of a girl on top of you, her hair framing her beautiful face; a young guy on his knees in front of you and he looks up and smiles–and I have felt a certain tenderness, have felt I want to just lie on a bed and talk to this person, share jokes, fantasies, share some time. A tenderness that while he is sucking me, she is thrusting her groin down on me, I think, this tenderness, this must lead to love. Then I blow, I come and the tenderness goes. Then all I want to do is go away. Put on my pants, wipe my dick and go away.

I ask myself how many people I've had sex with. I've lost count. I've become a slut.

They are playing bad Abba

They are playing bad Abba. *Dancing Queen.* I hate this song, I say to Con as we walk back in. Johnny and Crystal have moved from the bar and have found some seats near the entrance. Maria is with them, and a striking woman with platinum-coloured hair. The Abba song is playing but they have a Madonna video on the screen. A black and white video in which some Latino guy is licking her out.

I go up to Johnny and put my arm around him. A sign that I want a truce. Maria pecks me on the cheek and introduces me to her friend, Serena. Italian? I ask. Croatian, she replies. Johnny winks at me and whispers, no relation. Maria hears. Relation to who?

–A guy Johnny's been dating. I shuffle. Maria notices my frown. What's up? she asks.

–I hate this fucking song. Serena is asking Johnny what it's like dating a Croatian man. Johnny is weaving bullshit. Maria tells me I'll never make a good faggot. You hate Abba and love early Rolling Stones. She shakes her head at me. What kind of queer are you? Crystal giggles in my face. The Rolling Stones, he squeals, how boring.

–Early Stones, I correct him. Even more boring he replies. He is no longer friendly. Con comes up with both our drinks. Crystal glares at me. The Abba song is finishing and some good Detroit house comes blaring through the speakers. I grab Maria's arm and we move to the dance floor.

Dancing with Maria I can lose myself in the music. She is a smooth dancer, uses her hips, as if she can hear the call of the *tsiftiteli* in the music. To keep a rhythm with her I incorporate some belly dancing into my moves on the dance floor. She glides up to me, moving seductively around me. The other dancers are jumping around the floor, aerobic movements to the compelling beat. Maria and I ignore them. Another Madonna video is playing on the small TV monitors

that decorate the club. My eyes stray to the flickering images
on the screens. The song we are dancing to ends and Maria
grabs my hand. Who is the boy you came in with? she asks.

-Crystal's boyfriend. I leave it at that. He's cute, she tells
me. We are heading back to the table.

-You probably can have him. Maria laughs. Is he worth
it? she asks. I turn around to her. She presents an innocent
face to me. I don't answer, sit at the table next to Johnny
and gulp down my drink. I smell my hands. A strong odour
of semen. I wipe my hands on my jeans.

Serena is making conversation with Johnny, Maria is
chatting up Con, Crystal looks uncomfortable and I watch
music videos on the screen. A parade of faces pass by me,
I am being checked out, assessed, been given a score. I'm
doing the same thing. There is a party game Maria and I
play sometimes. Drunk, we'll scan the people in the room,
Yes, No, Maybe. Yes I'd sleep with him, No, I wouldn't sleep
with her, Maybe, if I was drunk enough. Most people are
Maybe. But neither she nor I am completely honest. Most
people are Yes but we don't acknowledge the truth because
we don't want to appear desperate. In a bed, with the lights
out, good drugs circulating through my body, I'll get a hard-
on with anyone.

Pubescent boys appear on the video screen, lip-synching.
They look like some of the boys wandering the club. Three
boys come up to Crystal and she starts squealing. A young
Thai boy in bicycle pants, a blond drunk boy heaped in
chains and hippie symbols, a black guy with his hair shaved
wearing a see-through silk shirt. The Thai boy keeps throwing
me glances. I avoid his eyes and concentrate on the screen.
I've done too much fucking already tonight. Part of me
would like to go home but I'm too wired from the drugs
and all I'd do would pace the bedroom floor and watch
music videos past dawn.

Maria is talking about some party, she's assuring Johnny
that it will be still raging. I know I want to move on, go

elsewhere, leave the dark insular club. I'll come, I tell her. Crystal introduces me to the three boys. I don't catch their names except for Rudy, the one with the see-through shirt. I ask him where he's from and he tells me Chicago. I tell him I'd like to go there one day. He's not very interested and I turn back to the screen. Maria tells him she has relatives in Chicago. Lots of Greeks in Chicago, aren't there? she asks. He looks bored. Maybe, he answers, I didn't hang out with them. I turn back to him. How come, I say aggressively, you a racist? He tenses up, his face hardens. I flash him a smile. Joke, I say. He smiles back and Crystal laughs. Rudy taps me on the shoulder and lowers his voice. I notice an erect nipple under the white silk of his shirt. A large purple nipple on a muscled chest. Crystal says you can get speed. How much do you want? I ask. He asks for a couple of grams, hands me the money and I go searching for Rat.

Rat is necking with a guy I don't recognise at the back of the club. I tap him on the shoulder, and we start a conversation. His pick-up for the night keeps kissing him, stroking his chest throughout the conversation. Some fucked-up blond Aussie guy; too many drugs, all he can focus on is Rat's body. I slip Rat the money and he slips me the drugs. The bank's closed, he tells me, you're the last customer. Rat goes back to his fuck and gives me a thumbs-up for a farewell. I take the two packets of drugs into the toilets and scoop a small amount of the powder onto my finger and snort it. Someone is getting fucked, or getting beaten in the next cubicle. Loud banging, soft groans. At the urinal a bald guy has his dick out. I wash my face and look into the mirror. My skin is stretched taut across my bones, my hair is wet, splattered across my forehead. I comb it back into place, gargle with some water and exit the toilets. I'm looking good.

I hand Rudy the drugs under the table. Crystal's friends immediately depart for the toilets. They ask me along but I'm not interested. Maria and Serena follow them into the

Ladies and I buy another drink. *Temptation* comes blaring through the speakers. My foot starts tapping and I get a speed rush. Wanna dance? I ask Johnny and Crystal, but they decline. I head off to the dance floor on my own. I'm in the middle of the crowd, swooping and shuffling to the song, raising my hands to the lights of disco Heaven. Rat and his boyfriend join me and Rat passes some amyl. Intoxicated, I dance with him while his boyfriend sways drunkenly, out of rhythm with the song, looking at himself in the full-length mirror at the back of the dance floor. When the amyl rush subsides I turn to Rat and ask where he picked him up. He's a bit of a dickhead, I say. Rat throws me a pretend punch, lightly knocking my chin, and tells me to shut up. They're all dickheads here, he shouts. I keep dancing till the end of the song, slap Rat's palm farewell and head back to the table. Maria and Serena are back. The boys are still in the toilet.

   –Let's go, I say, let's get out of here. Johnny asks Maria if she'll drop him off home and she agrees. Crystal wants to stay. I shake Con's hand. A strong, masculine handshake. See you around, he says. Sure, I answer. I'm impatient to go. The bouncers open the doors for me and I'm into the night. The hot-dog stand is still there, so are the taxis. The cool night air strokes my flesh. I no longer want the night to end. Home is the last place I want to be.

SOUTH

Pet Shop Boys *Being boring*

Another world

Another world is unfolding outside the club. The man at the hot-dog stall is talking about his girlfriend to one of the taxi drivers. A drunk teenage couple are walking down the street, the boy supporting his staggering girlfriend. They stop for a hot dog and the girl goes on a rave about how much she likes dancing with gay men. Australian men can't dance, she tells the hot-dog man and his driver friend, they can't fucking dance for shit. Poofters can dance. Her boyfriend tells her to shut up.

I wander across the street from the club, looking into the windows of the taxi cabs. Some of the drivers are hanging out, looking desperate. They're waiting to pick up some stray fag from the club, someone who couldn't get a fuck. Someone who'll suck them off down by the river. I light a cigarette and look at bored faces. They ignore me. In one cab two Greek drivers are playing cards in the front. I stand and watch them. One of them rolls down the window and asks me what the fuck do I want. Nothing, I answer and walk back to the door of the club. A police van crawls slowly past the strip. The drunk girl starts to yell abuse at them. Shut the fuck up her boyfriend hisses at her and shakes her a little. The hot-dog man, the driver, we all look away. Maria, Serena and Johnny join me on the steps. The girl starts giggling at Johnny. Honey, you're beautiful, she jeers. Johnny gives her a dagger look. Honey, you're a mess, he replies. Fucking faggot, she calls out and nestles under her boyfriend's arm. We head off to Maria's car.

Fucking faggot

Fucking faggot rings in my ear. Faggot I don't mind. I like the word. I like queer, I like the Greek word *pousti*. I hate the word gay. Hate the word homosexual. I like the word wog, can't stand dago, ethnic or Greek-Australian. You're either Greek or Australian, you have to make a choice. Me, I'm neither. It's not that I can't decide; I don't like definitions.

If I was black I'd call myself nigger. It's strong, scary, loud. I like it for the same reasons I like the words cocksucker and wog. If I was Asian I'd call myself a gook, but I'd use it loudly and ferociously so it scares whitey. Use it to show whitey that it's not all yes-sir-no-sir-we-Asians-work-hard-good-capitalists-do-anything-the-white-man-says-sir. Wog, nigger, gook. Cocksucker. Use them right, the words have guts.

Her words, fucking faggot, they ring in my ear.

In the car

In the car Greek music with a middle-eastern tinge is playing. Maria shakes her hips as she drives. I'm in the front, hanging my head out the window to feel the breeze. An old drunk on the steps of the Masonic Hospital waves to me. I wave back. In the back Johnny's complaining about the music. What's this wog shit, Maria? he calls out. Put something else on. Maria ignores him, she turns up the volume. Johnny screeches from the back. Take off that fucking song, he yells. I keep staring out the window, ignoring the racket inside the car.

We stop at the Seven Eleven on Punt Road and Maria and I get out to get cigarettes. As soon as we are out of the car Johnny switches off the tape. Inside the store the humming of electricity, the throbbing of the refrigerators interacts with the neurons in my head and I'm overwhelmed by the bright fluorescent lights. A bored young Indian guy serves us, not looking at us. He hands over three packets of cigarettes and we hand over the money. I look at the dry pies and sausage rolls on display, tempted to have something to eat, but my hunger tonight is all in the head. My stomach feels full and I decide against food. My lips are dry and I want another drink. No alcohol is being sold.

Out on the street Johnny has some crap plastic commercial radio music blaring from the stereo. When we are back in the car I turn off the radio and put the tape back in. I hear Johnny snarling at me from the back but I don't catch his words. Not that it matters. He is tired, drunk, off his face and looks like he needs some sleep. Serena tries to make conversation with him but he doesn't reply to her questions.

I'm glad when we reach his house. I get out, open the door for him and he takes my arm. I walk him to his front door. Lights are still on and there is a faint sound of music coming from inside the house. He groans and puts his arms around me. Ari, he croons into my ear, I hope that the old man hasn't got some old whore in there with him.

–You want me to come in? I ask. He shakes his head and plants a wet kiss on my mouth. You go and party, he tells me, and pinches my butt. I'll deal with Papa. He releases me and fumbles at the lock with his key. I forgive you for tonight he tells me as he opens the door. Sure, I answer. I can't remember if I've done anything to be forgiven for, can't remember if he should be apologising to me. It doesn't matter much. It doesn't matter at all.

In the dim light of the hall Johnny's father is staring at us, drunk, in boxer shorts and a singlet. I say hello *theo*, and he grunts and comes and shakes my hand. He ignores his son. Where you off to? he asks me. A party. He wipes his mouth with his arm and tells me to have a good time, fuck a few sheilas for him. Sure, I reply wanting to leave, not wanting to get into a conversation with a drunk. Johnny waves goodbye to me and I walk away. Fuck a few *palikaria* for me, Johnny calls out. He and his father start a loud argument and I get into the car. Drive, drive away, I tell Maria and she foots the accelerator. She turns down the volume on the stereo and tells me Johnny is giving her the shits. He's too

demanding, he's a selfish prick. We are approaching the
river and the large billboard on top of the silos announces
it is three thirty in the morning, it is nineteen degrees in the
city. A warm night. I light a cigarette for myself, one for
Maria and hand one to Serena.

-Where's the party? I ask. Prahran, Maria answers and
takes the cigarette. Maria can tell I don't want to talk about
Johnny and changes the subject. There's some stash in the
glovebox she tells me, roll us a joint. I obey and Serena
leans forward and asks how Johnny's father copes with
having a drag for a son. Maria gives a loud laugh. He's a
wog, she calls out, what would you reckon your old man
would say if your brother came home in a dress?

-My father would kill him

-No he wouldn't, I tell her. He'd have to learn to live with
it. I start putting the joint together. My father would kill him,
Serena insists, he's Croatian.

-In which case, Maria tells her, since he's Croatian he'd
probably fuck him first. Then he'd kill him. And then fuck
him again. I laugh and drop some grass on the car floor.
Serena says, oh yuck, and sits back.

-Which is exactly what Johnny's father did, Maria continues. My gut hardens. I don't like Johnny's life exposed to
some stranger. Serena leans forward again. Seriously? she
asks.

-Seriously, Maria replies, ain't that so, Ari? I don't answer,
concentrate on the joint. Wogs can't keep their mouths shut,
can't keep their noses out of people's business. Young, old,
male, female, dumb, smart. Gossip is essential to conversation.
It makes for lack of trust. I hear what Maria says about
Johnny, what she exposes about his life when he's not here,
and then I wonder what she says about me when I'm not
there. I keep my mouth shut.

-That's sick. Serena states her condemnation emphatically.
I lick the gum on the tobacco paper and roll the mix into
a small joint. I light it and take a deep draw.

-It's abuse, Maria agrees. A cop car is turning into High Street and I hide the joint under the dashboard, pass it to Maria. When the cops turn, she brings it to her lips. The dope has an immediate effect. I relax back into the seat. The song playing on the stereo is sad, melancholy. Exquisitely painful. A few times Johnny enjoyed the sex with his old man, I want to say. Instead I ask Maria about the song.

-It's Greek-Macedonian, she tells me, beautiful isn't it?

-Can you understand it? Serena asks. What's it about? I strain to listen to the lyrics. My Greek isn't good enough. Maria translates the lyrics.

-A young girl is getting married and she's really sad about having to leave her village. Oh mother, she is saying, when will I see you again? Serena laughs. It sounds more beautiful when you don't understand the lyrics. I'm dying to leave my mother. Maria agrees. She parks in front of an old block of flats and switches off the stereo. The lament drops dead in mid-aria. In a small courtyard a group of people are sitting in a half-circle passing a bottle of alcohol around. Party still going, Maria says happily. Serena butts the joint and we get out of the car.

I'm still tripping

I'm still tripping. The crowd of people on the lawn, their faces hidden in darkness, cast weird long shadows that move in the breeze, forming independent shapes that do not match the bodies that have spawned them. I put my arm around Maria and we walk up some concrete steps. The door to an apartment is half open and dance music is being played at a soft volume. I feel like another dance.

The party is dying. Not dead yet, but instead of a large crowd, there are clusters of people sitting around on couches, in corners of a large white lounge room. Two guys, mid-twenties, in tight shorts and leather vests are dancing aggressively to the dance beat. I head towards the kitchen in search of drink. In the kitchen two women in black with heavy make-up are smoking a joint. A burly man is sitting on a bench sipping a can of beer. I make for the refrigerator and search for something to take my thirst away. I find nothing.

-What are you looking for? one of the women asks me. Something to drink, I reply. It's bring your own, she tells me, and gives me a dirty look. I ignore her and search along the bench. I find a half-full bottle of brandy, and pour a large serve into a plastic cup. The woman shakes her head at me and I put on an aggressive face. She ignores me and the man starts making some conversation with me. The acid, however, seems to be on a second peak and I have difficulty catching his words. I sit next to him on the bench and wait for the intense throbbing in my head to pass. Across from me on the wall hangs a print of a Japanese temple. I stare at it and swear I can see birds flying across the sky. The man is still talking to me and the music in the next room seems to be getting louder. A heavy monotonous rap. I hear one of the women saying, he's really out of it. I feel the man put an arm around me and I haven't got the energy to push him away. His arm feels heavy on my shoulder. What are you on? I hear. I can't tell who is asking me, the man or one of the women. I take a large sip of brandy and it burns. I believe I can feel it washing through into my stomach. I look up and Maria and Serena have come into the room.

The man takes his arm away from me and kisses Maria. He introduces her to the women. I don't catch any names. I hear him ask if I'm alright. Maria comes over and gently caresses my face. You okay, Ari? she asks. I blink and I feel near normal. Or rather I feel more speedy than trippy. I'm fine, I tell the group in the kitchen. Let's dance.

-In a minute, Maria says and takes a seat. I pour some more brandy in the glass. Are you at college, Ari? the man asks me. I shake my head.

-Do you study? I shake my head.

-Are you working? I shake my head. One of the women in black asks me if I'm an artist of some sort. I shake my head. Too many questions. They give up on their interrogation and go back to a conversation about books, about university. I'm bored and get up and go into the lounge room. On the couch a large, good-looking older man in a tuxedo has his arms around a young Japanese boy. The boy is playing with the man's trouser buttons. I can't help looking at them and the older man winks at me. He pats the space beside him on the couch and I turn away and head towards the stereo. I'm not interested in taking part in some multicultural orgy. I'm conscious that I look good, attractive, and that most of the men in the room are looking at me. So are some of the women. I like the attention. I'm strutting as I walk towards the stereo.

No one is dancing. A pile of CDs are on the floor. I look through them. Seventies disco and eighties techno. I crouch by the stereo and look through the CDs lined up against the shelves. There are dozens and dozens of them. I'm in some rich cunt's apartment. The matt-black stereo is new, no dust anywhere. A large television against the lounge-room wall is playing music videos with the sound turned off. I flick through the CDs, past classical music, past opera, past ballet music. Serena comes and joins me. The music has stopped and someone calls out for me to put something on. I trace the line of CDs with my finger and search for something I like. I'm having difficulty finding anything. Serena finds *Abba's Greatest Hits* and wants to play it. I refuse. I refuse again. Just *Knowing Me, Knowing You* she asks. I relent. That's one Abba song I can stand. We put it on and I keep searching through the CDs. Serena lies against the wall and sings along to the lyrics. She looks despondent and I leave the CDs and ask her if she's feeling well. She doesn't answer, continues singing the chorus and doesn't look at me. I turn away and look around the room. Ari. I hear her call my name. I'm in love with your friend Maria.

I don't answer. Maria has never told me anything about sleeping with women, but I know she's a flirt. She's Greek. We all flirt. Serena goes back to singing the song. Her pale hair, her pale skin, the dark luminous eyes. She looks beautiful and she looks sad. The song ends and I light a cigarette. What do you want to hear? I ask her. I take off the CD and Serena searches through the stack. Play some metal. I groan. Don't you like it? she asks. She looks hurt. Metal's alright, I answer, and I sift through the CDs. There is nothing hardcore in the collection but I manage to find a Guns N' Roses CD single, *Sweet Child O' Mine*, which I quite like. I put it on. Maria comes into the room and laughs at hearing the song. Reminds me of high school, she hisses at us and joins Serena in the dance. I watch them dancing, watch them scream the chorus to each other. I hum along softly. A few people in the room are looking at the dancing women with frustration, they don't like the music.

The song ends and a thrashier, more furious metal number begins. Serena puts her arms around Maria's neck and starts kissing her softly across her face. Maria is pulling away. I go back to the kitchen, refill my glass with the last of the brandy and go back into the lounge, rest my back against a wall and watch Serena dancing. Maria has sat down, is flicking through the CDs. One of the boys in leather and shorts is asking her to take off this metal shit and put some dance music on. I watch Serena shake her head to the music, her body responds hungrily to the screeching guitars. She is the music; losing herself in it.

I straighten up, go over to Maria and order her to leave the song on till it's finished. The boy puts his hands on his hips and tells me that this is his party and he'll play whatever the fuck he wants. I push him aside. Push him hard. I'm angry. I'm not sure why, but I'm ready to smash my fist into the face of the arsehole in front of me. Serena comes over and takes my hand, starts dancing with me. She screams the chorus to me and I scream back at her. I'm making up words. The song ends and we pull apart.

I look over to the couch and the Japanese boy, still playing with his boyfriend's cock, is looking at us. He doesn't look legal, does he? I ask Serena and she looks over at the duo on the couch. She pulls away from me. The world stinks don't it Ari? she tells me, the world is fucked up, isn't it? Sure, I say softly and I light a cigarette. But he looks like he's on good drugs, I continue, he looks happy.

Some records

Some records everybody has. As a kid in the playground, when all you knew about music is what you heard on the radio and what you saw on television, Abba reigned supreme. And T-Rex. Having an older brother I also got to listen to Deep Purple (always hated them). Having a mother into music meant I also got to hear the Rolling Stones and the Animals (there is an old photo of my father in a work uniform at the General Motors factory at Fishermen's Bend and he looks like Eric Burdon, but darker, woggier). When we were children Alex and I bashed each other up in a record shop over whether to buy the soundtrack to *Grease* or the soundtrack to *Star Wars*. I wanted *Star Wars*. She wanted *Grease*. She won.

Everyone had Fleetwood Mac's *Tusk*. In high school everyone had Pink Floyd's *The Wall*. And Michael Jackson's *Off the Wall*. My brother had *Never Mind the Bollocks*. Alex bought *Thriller*. I bought the first Depeche Mode. Peter still listens to the first Birthday Party album and gave me *Nick the Stripper* for my thirteenth birthday. I gave Johnny Bronski Beat for a birthday, he gave me *Yo Bum Rush the Show*. All of Alex's girlfriends had Van Halen's *1984*. My mother bought Culture Club and the Eurythmics.

Dad only bought Greek music and a few Elvis records. For a while you couldn't go to a party, any party, without hearing De La Soul.

I can't recite you a poem, any poem, but my mind is an automatic memory teller of pop music.

Everyone has Madonna. Call her a tramp. My mum does. Call her a slut. All the boys at school did. Call her a bad singer. As if it matters. But everyone has a Madonna record. She was the first woman I saw who showed off her cunt with as much bravado and pride as a man showed off his dick. Bootlegged Madonna tapes, sent over by penpals from Australia must be like hard currency on the streets of Tehran. I keep thinking of some young girl in full chador, her veil covering her Walkman, walking down a street, ignored by all these Muslim men, and she's listening to *Like a Virgin*, or *Justify My Love*. And going home, alone in her bedroom, touching her cunt, liking it. Bless the Madonna.

I go over to the boy in shorts. Put on some Madonna? I ask him, and then add, Sorry for getting aggro before. Not too loud, not making too big a deal of it. He smiles at me. That's more like it, he tells me and flicks through the CDs. He bends over and I catch a glimpse of fine blond hair running up the back of his thighs, disappearing under the thin black lycra pulled tight around his round arse. I finish my drink and go to the toilet, pissing through a half-stiff cock.

Everyone gets up

Everyone gets up to dance. To Madonna's *Holiday*. Maria is dancing with the man in the tuxedo. Serena is dancing with his young boyfriend. The burly man and the two women from the kitchen come into the lounge room and form a triangle. The music is on loud and everyone is singing along. The music pounds into my eardrums and I walk away from

the frenzied dance into a small hallway and push open a
door. A small bedroom. I jump on the bed and flick on the
bedside light. In front of me there sits a small TV. Beside
me is the remote control and I flick the screen on. Flick
through the channels. Heavy metal music clips. Flick past
that. Ads. Flick past them. Peter O'Toole and Audrey
Hepburn in *How to Steal a Million*. I sit back on the pillows
and turn up the volume. Madonna is still audible. I turn up
the volume louder and watch the movie. O'Toole at his
most handsome, Hepburn at her prettiest. The world on
the screen is much more attractive than the world I move
around in. I lower my head on my chest and breathe deeply.
I'm too tired to sleep, too mindfucked to keep partying.
There is a knock on the door. Come in, I mumble.

George comes into the room. I'm hallucinating. George
comes into the room. I am not hallucinating. I want to
straighten up, I can't and instead I lower my head again. A
young boy is behind him, the one I pushed around. I'm
trying to straighten up, can't do it. I feel fucking fantastic
seeing him, realise I have had him in the back of my thoughts
all night. I also realised I'm pissed off to see him obviously
friendly with the pansy-boy. I can almost hate him for that.
George comes over and grabs my hand. He seems glad to
see me. His presence in the room is overpowering. I smell
him. I smell him all over me, he is soaking through my skin.
He sits beside me on the bed, and asks me if I'm out of it.
No, I'm fine, I glower. The boy looks down on me. You
know each other? he asks.

–I live with his brother. George introduces me to the boy.
I don't give a fuck, don't even try and listen to the name. I
look up and George is smiling at me. His hair gelled, his
face shaven; he is luminous. The boy offers George a joint
and he lights it, takes a couple of drags and offers it to me.
I inhale deeply. I fumble in my jeans pocket for my cigarettes.
They are there. I pass the joint along. The boy takes two,
three long drags, gives it to George and then gets up. Come

and dance soon, I hear him say. I don't look up as he leaves the room. The door shuts. I relax a little, glad he is out of here. I look up at George who is staring at the TV screen. I tense up again.

–A good movie, is it? he asks me. Yeah, I reply. I've seen it before. He asks me who the actor is and I'm disappointed. He doesn't know Peter O'Toole.

–Been here long? No, I answer. I keep watching the TV, watch Audrey and Peter flirting with each other, making light conversation. Falling in love. George passes me the joint and I want to touch his neck, feel his skin. Is that your girlfriend inside? he asks me.

–Who?

–The Greek girl. He means Maria. No, just a friend. The question pisses me off. Peter must have kept quiet about his little brother sleeping with men. It is something Peter doesn't talk about much.

My body is taut, I am tight all over. My T-shirt is constricting me. I finish the joint and he takes it from me, brushes my hand. I see sparks, a tiny shower of electricity rains down on the bed from the point where our hands touched. He sees nothing. He butts out the joint in an ashtray and watches the movie. I guess we should go inside, he says. No, I say loudly. I want to stay here. He doesn't move.

–I find you very attractive, Ari. He does not look at me as he tells me. And I'm very stoned. He gets up from the bed and turns around to me. Sorry, he says softly, I shouldn't have said that. I pull my knees up tight against my chest and concentrate furiously on the screen. Words are forming, whole sentences are at play at the tip of my tongue. Nothing comes out. I'm grinding hard on my teeth. See you, Ari.

–Stay, I bark it out. He doesn't leave but he doesn't sit down. I light a cigarette and he asks for one. I hand it over and he lightly touches my hand, runs his fingers up my naked arm. I hold it out to him, close my eyes. He touches my face, a light touch, caressing me. Have you done it with a guy before, Ari? Then he laughs. A sarcastic laugh. He takes his hand away. I guess you have, he says.

His words are knives. Carving me up. I fix my eyes on the screen. In his eyes I am something else, I am someone else. I'm a wog boy, a straight boy. He is blind to my desire for him. I feel naive, vulnerable. But in my head, running around and around and around is the thought that I must appear strong for him to want me. He too wants the one hundred percent genuine wog fuck.

He sits down next to me and I still can't look at him. He butts out the half-smoked cigarette. I look at him. He's boyish but not soft. I want to tell him I adore him but the words don't come out. He is nervous and that touches me. I pull him to me and we are kissing.

I feed on his mouth, I fall into him. He kisses me all over my face, my neck, pulls my T-shirt over my chest and licks my nipples. I lie back and he pulls down my zip, and my dick is rock hard as he takes it in his mouth. I push hard into his mouth. I'm silent. He tries to pull away from my cock and I hold tight onto his head, forcing my cock deeper into his throat. The room has disappeared. The thrusts don't last long. There is a pounding in my head, the whole world is trapped inside me, the whole world consists of George and myself. I hold my breath and release the world. Three quick thrusts and I come. He pulls away, spits into the bedsheet and wipes his mouth. He is furious. He leans over me. My wet cock is still hard. He pulls down his jeans and forces my hand on his cock.

I want to clean myself up but he won't let me. He grips hard on my hand, his nails biting into my flesh. Suck me, Ari, he orders. I don't make a move. He lets go of my hand, and sits on my chest pushing his cock in my face. I turn away and he pulls at my hair until my lips are rubbing against the cock head. He pushes into my mouth and I choke as his cock is forced down my throat. I raise myself onto the bed and lick his cock and massage his balls. He groans and strokes my hair and I take his cock further and further into my mouth, saliva dribbles down my cheeks, I still feel as if I'm choking yet it is impossible for me to release him. He comes and lets out an anguished groan. I swallow all of his come, swallow the shit he flushes down my throat, lick his cock, his balls, his groin, swallow his sweat and his semen and his flesh. He tries to pull away but I don't let him, keep his cock deep in my mouth until he is wincing. He pulls away violently. A drop of fluid falls on my cheek. He wipes his cock with the sheet and lies down next to me. My fists are two tight balls, I'm crushing my own fingers. The sex is over.

George lights me a cigarette. I take it and look down at my body, my cock hanging out, my T-shirt stained. I don't care. I smoke the cigarette, smelling the stink of semen, sweat and nicotine. Miami Sound Machine is on the stereo in the party room. George says something to me. I turn around. He wipes a line of sweat from my brow. I flinch as he touches me. Peter is kissing Audrey on the screen. Too many sounds, images, movements. Turn that fucking thing off, I ask him. He gets up and switches it off and sits down on the bed. There is a knock on the door and he throws the sheet over my body. I couldn't care, couldn't care who sees me, dick hanging out, dripping come. Maria pokes her head in the room. You want to leave, Ari? she asks. She comes in.

–No, I'll stay. We can wait, she says. I shake my head. She comes over to kiss me goodbye. I don't move. Her lips feel cold on my cheek. She smooths back my hair and leaves the room without looking at George. She turns back and asks if I'm sure I'll be alright to get home.

–I'll take him home. George smiles at her and, hesitantly, Maria smiles back at him. She says goodbye again, this time in Greek and I don't answer, watch her walk out of the room. She shuts the door behind her.

George lies next to me, his face near mine and rubs his hand along my chest. I smoke the cigarette, watch the smoke form ghosts in the air. You are so good-looking, Ari, he whispers to me.

–And you're fucking gorgeous. I say it and let out a sigh. I've got the words out. You think so? he asks me, a wide grin on his face. Yeah, sure, I answer, for a guy. I'm using words as a shield, protecting myself. I don't know who he wants me to be. I don't know who I want him to be. He stops smiling.

–Do you want me to leave? No, I answer. Do you want me to take you home? Again, I shake my head, no. He looks frustrated. I glance at the alarm clock on the bedside table. Maybe I should go home. Whatever time I get home there is going to be a fight with Mum or Dad. Probably both. I want to ask to forget the sex, the way I feel about him, to ask him to forget I am my brother's brother. I want him to stop asking questions and I want him and me to never leave this room. Dawn will be coming up soon. I groan. Mum is going to kill me, I tell him.

–So you want me to take you home? No, fuck you, I yell, I don't want you to take me home.

–You just said … He stops mid-sentence. He sits on the bed. I give up, he continues and lights another cigarette and sucks on it hard, all you Greeks are liars. I laugh at him.

–It's true. Whenever someone rings up for your brother I have to pretend I've just gotten up or just come home. He begins miming that he is talking on the telephone. No Mrs Voulis, I don't know where Peter is, he must be at the library. Studying. I go to my brother's defence.

–You just have to lie, I tell George. Bullshit. He says it hard, spittle flies towards me. All it takes is guts, confront your parents. It is your life after all. I listen to his words. I've heard them before; I've played them in my own head, played them over and over. You have to lie, I repeat. He starts to say something and I continue to speak over him, I continue to get my words out. Try not to think about how they sound.

–You have to lie, maybe not all the time, and maybe there are some things you can't lie about but most things aren't worth the effort. I'll lie about where I'm going, I'll lie about who I'm with, I'll lie about what I've been doing if I think it will save an argument,' save some time. I look at the fine blond hairs forming webs across George's chest. I begin to falter in my words. I want to reach a finger out to him, touch him, put his fingers to my mouth, to taste him. You might think it funny, I tell him, all these lies and stories and arguments over the phone. But I don't think they're funny, they're just boring. It's easier to lie.

–You just have to tell the truth once. George gets on his knees, his face is close to mine. I smell the aftershave, the nicotine, the alcohol. Just once, Ari, once you tell them the truth, one argument, no matter how brutal and you never have to lie again.

–You're wrong. I look straight into his blue eyes. Foreign eyes. I can see the sky in them. You're wrong, I speak to his eyes. Truth they use against you. I speak slowly, no mumbling, no slurring. I struggle to form my words free of the deleterious effects of the drugs, of my emotions. You're wrong, you never tell a wog anything important about yourself. The truth is yours, it doesn't belong to no one else.

–And so you never grow up. George is still over me. Always little children, never adults. I don't say anything to him, just stare into his face, look bored. This angers him. He grabs tight onto my wrists. Don't you ever, don't you ever want to be free of the hold they have over you? Fuck, don't you ever want to grow up?

–You talking about my parents or your parents? I say it laconically, I spice my tone with arrogance. He relaxes his grip on my wrists. I curl my right hand into a fist and slam it hard into his stomach. Hard, so hard that he stops breathing for a moment, then squeals and falls on me. All my anger I put into my fist, all my anguish I throw into the punch.

George falls on me, tears in his eyes, gasping for breath. I watch his head on my chest, watch him slowly rise up onto his knees again. He hits at me, no punches, a slap on the side of my head. He kicks his knee into my thigh. He's thrashing around like a little child, the tears still falling from his eyes. I can't feel the pain. From somewhere deep inside me I hear a faint word being repeated again and again. The word is sorry. It sounds like it's coming from a long, long way off. Further than the next room, almost imperceptible. It slowly gains volume and then the words crash into the room and I see George on top of me, hitting me and I hear myself yelling I'm sorry, I'm sorry.

–I don't believe a word you say, you fucking arsehole he shouts into my ear. I lie still. Do you like me? Ari? Do you want to sleep with me again? His face is still white with anger. I'm looking into his eyes and for the first time in my life I look at angry blue eyes. Heat, ferocious heat, is blue. Yes. I tell him yes. He lets go of me. Lights a cigarette.

–You're a nice young kid, Ari, fucked up but that's normal. He passes me the cigarette. You're a nice kid. Find yourself a good Greek girl, Ari, that's what you really want, eh? Stop messing around with us poofters. Go home to Mummy and Daddy, go where you fucking belong. He wipes his face with a handkerchief, tucks his shirt into his trousers, runs a hand through his hair. He smiles down to me. I want to punch his fucking face in.

–Should I take you home, Ari? he asks me. I laugh. No mate, I tell him, butting out the cigarette, putting my clothes back on. I smile at him, but keep clear of him. If we were to touch, if I was to be close to him again I could kill him. Are you sure you don't want me to take you home, it's on the way? I refuse again. He stands, a nervous smile, looking like a little kid. He hesitates, wondering whether to shake my hand goodbye, kiss my mouth, my cheek. I sit still and watch him, finally, walk away. Yo, George, I want to call out, I'm wrong, you're wrong, the whole fucking world is wrong.

I love you. I want to say the words, but they are an obscenity I can't bring myself to mouth. I've never said those words. I'm never going to say those words. I watch him walk out the door. He doesn't look back.

Lyrics run in my head. *You can't look back*, you can never look back. I stare at my reflection on the blank screen, I pick up the remote from the floor and turn onto a music video. A long-haired, scarred-skin young boy is screaming into a microphone. No sound. Kylie Minogue is singing in the lounge room. I leave the volume off, sink back into the pillow and do my own screaming. Not one sound comes out of my mouth.

The smell of the sea

The smell of the sea tickles my nose. Through the half-open window of the room I am in I can hear echoes of the waves hitting the shoreline of St Kilda Beach. The beach which for decades has been the home of junkies and whores, refugees and migrants, now being redone, remodelled, restructured into a playground for the sophisticated professional. Under the piers, in toilets, in the back of discos, St Kilda offered me in my youth a smorgasbord of illicit pleasures. Cheap drugs, free sex. Getting drunk, getting stoned, getting high.

The sea breeze tickles my nose. Along the coastline of the city, the beaches open up to the chasm which is the end of the world. Below us there is ice. Nothing else. No human life, no villages, no towns, no cities. Many nights I would take the tram and head down the beach, walk along the sand and sit on the end of the pier looking out to the darkness of the bay and dream of what I could find if I dived into the waves and swam away. Looking out to the horizon, I would dream of new places, new faces, new lives possible to live at the other side of the world. Never thoughts of ice, instead I thought of the North, the places my mother and father talked to me about. The arid soil and hot weather of the Mediterranean.

The Greeks, sons of sailors, daughters of fishwives. Rarely rich enough to live next to the sea, the Greeks live one suburb away. Never close enough to the bay to receive the strong sea gales straight into the lungs; just close enough to allow the breeze to tickle the nose.

To the South are the wogs who have been shunted out of their communities. Artists and junkies and faggots and whores, the sons and daughters no longer talked about, no longer admitted into the arms of family. In the South, in the flats and apartments smelling of mildew and mice, are all the wog rejects from the North, the East, the West. Flushed out towards the sea. When you look straight across the ocean you look into the face of your dreams.

The whore dominates the imagination of the Greek, of the Turk, of the Arab. The insults my father threw at me when I first challenged his authority were words meant for a woman. *Poutana, skula.* Whore, dog. His one English obscenity. Cunt. Those insults have formed me, they have nourished me. In latrines and underneath piers I have enjoyed pleasures that are made sweeter by the contempt I know they bestow on me in the eyes of the respectable world I abhor. And the danger I face in pursuing my pleasures is the guarantee I have that I am not forsaking my masculinity. The constraints placed on me by my family can only be destroyed by a debasement that allows me to run along dark paths and silent alleyways forbidden to most of my clan and my peers. To be free, for me as a Greek, is to be a whore. To resist the path of marriage and convention, of tradition and obedience, I must make myself an object of derision and contempt. Only then am I able to move outside the suffocating obligations of family and loyalty.

That I am a whore, a dog, a cunt, is no one's business. To confess my life, or even to proclaim it proudly, entraps me in an interaction with the wogs which would draw me back within the suffocating circle. My silence and my secrets allow me to move freely around the landscape of my city. A public life is a privilege only available to the rich, to the famous.

The sea breeze of the southern ocean, the breeze that comes up from the end of the world, makes me strong, draws me to the whores and faggots and junkies. I am a sailor and a whore. I will be till the end of the world.

I'm coming down

I'm coming down. I can't lift my head off the pillow and I try to light a cigarette. A lifetime passes in reaching for the cigarette. A lifetime passes in bringing it to my mouth. A lifetime passes in lighting it. I inhale the smoke to stop my teeth from grinding on each other. On the television monitor I watch flickering images: a woman in a miniskirt, a man in leather, a beachscape, the bombing of Baghdad, a burial in Sarajevo, mushroom clouds, desert, a couple kissing, guns, the Virgin Mary, the red crescent, the hammer and sickle, silence = death, the US flag, tits, bums, crotch shots, guns, another mushroom cloud. Young black guys pointing fat fingers towards me, white guys spitting at my face; women licking their lips shoving their arses towards me. I forget the cigarette in my hand and it burns my finger. I let it fall on the bed, watch the sheet begin to burn and struggle to lift my head, exercise my dry mouth to produce some saliva and spit a gob onto the burning hole. I lift myself off the bed and stumble across the room, falling onto a chair.

Slowly, step by fucking step, concentrating on my feet, I walk out and into a dim hallway. Dawn light is visible. Janet Jackson is on the stereo in the lounge room. I search for the bathroom and find it, a small room lit by fluorescent light. In the mirror I look at my skin, at the dark blotches forming around my still too-wide eyes. My hair is standing on end. I close the door and wash myself thoroughly, take off my T-shirt and wash away the thin, white residue of George's sperm on my body; wash away my sweat, his sweat, my come, his come. Wash away all traces of smell on my body.

I wash myself so hard till my body is red raw. I take out my cock and scrub it, wash out the dried come forming under the foreskin, wash away the traces of his saliva on my cockhead. When I am done, I wipe my body with a dirty towel hanging over the shower rail and comb my hair back into shape. I walk out the bathroom and walk into the lounge room. Three people are sitting in a circle smoking bongs. I take a couple of pipes but I am silent. They in turn do not ask me questions. They offer their smoke out of drug etiquette. After all, I have partied till dawn.

After my third pipe I get up on unsteady legs and wave goodbye. They don't lift their heads. I search my pockets for my cigarettes and I can't find them. I go back into the bedroom and search there, find them on the bedside table and I decide to open the drawer to have a look. Some condoms, a pocketbook, some tapes and a Walkman. A Sony Walkman in good condition. I take it out and cradle it under my arm. I take a hurried look through the tapes. Nothing I like except an old Beastie Boys cassette. I pocket it. I light a cigarette and walk through the house and out the door. No one looks at me while I'm leaving; no one notices the Walkman under my arm. The sun has risen and the street is glowing in warm summer colours. I sniff hard and I can almost taste the sea, somewhere behind all the flats, all the concrete.

I stand outside till my cigarette is finished and then put one foot ahead of the other. I hook the earphones on and press the play button on the Walkman. A beautiful clear sound. An expensive piece of machinery, but the tape inside is shit-awful, polished contemporary soul lacking any heart and any spirit. Some white man trying to pretend to be black or some black guy completely castrated by the dictates of the music business and the pop charts. I take off the tape and throw it in a bush. I take out the Beastie Boys cassette from my back pocket and put it in. A deafening crash of drums and guitar enters my eardrums and I'm no longer coming down. I turn up the volume and walk towards home.

WEST

Nirvana *Smells like teen spirit*

Mum and Dad

Mum and Dad are going to kill me. I'm not thinking about George, I'm not thinking about the party, I'm not thinking about the weather, I'm not thinking about sleep. The Walkman is screaming at me that I have to fight for my right to party and all I can think of is that Mum and Dad are going to kill me. I increase the pace of my walking and walk down Chapel Street towards home. I pass Italian boys in white shirts setting up seats outside their cafes and cross High Street and watch old Greek couples head off to church or maybe to the market. People get out of my way.

The Beastie Boys are singing about hard cocks and girls with ever-ready pussy. Slowly, slowly, thoughts of Mum and Dad recede. Glimpses of George in my mind. His cock, half-erect, the hair covering his chest, the roll of flesh around his stomach. The speed and the acid and the eckie and the grog and the dope are still running around my system. I cross Commercial Road, cross Toorak Road and take the path down to the river. A group of private school boys in singlets and shorts are going rowing. All golden hair, muscles and tanned skin. I ignore them and head for the nearest toilet, under the bridge. I piss, a long piss, into the metal urinal and when I'm finished I wait there, standing with my cock hanging out. I still have the Walkman on, but I've turned down the volume.

A tall guy with shaved hair, wearing a black T-shirt and leather pants, enters the toilet and stands at the urinal next to me. He doesn't take a piss. I would prefer to get off with a wog but I'm horny and I want some sex to forget George (to forget his pale skin) and this guy will have to do. He takes out his cock and starts masturbating. I start pulling myself. He puts his hand on my cock and tugs hard. I can hear him mouth something but I keep the Walkman on.

He removes the left earphone and whispers if I want to come home with him. I refuse and put the earphone back. Metal rap comes out of the headphones. He keeps tugging at himself and at me. It is taking ages for me to come. A sound behind us makes us stop and we stand apart.

Some old Yugoslav guy with a big gut and grey hair is stroking his crotch. I turn around to him and show him my cock. He takes his out and I go over and we start wanking. The man in the leather pants comes over as well but I ignore him now. The old man has a huge thick cock that he has trouble getting up. The foreskin is pulled tight around the cockhead. He starts kissing me and I resist, draw away from him, but I let him touch me all over, let his fingers go up my arsehole. He smells of cheap aftershave. Metal rap is pounding in my ears. I want him to come all over me, in my mouth, to wipe away all traces of George. But he doesn't try to get me to suck him off. Instead, the shaved-head guy gets on his knees and is sucking us both, taking turns.

I put my hands inside the old man's shirt and rub his chest; thick and heavy tits, fat hairy gut. He tries to kiss me again and I move away and wank myself, close to coming. I ejaculate all over the faggot on his knees, come falling on his cheeks, his lips, on his torso. The Yugoslav guy reaches for me, trying to get me to jerk him. I'm no longer interested. I push away his hand and walk out of the toilet into the green park. I'm dripping come into my underwear. I can no longer smell George on me. I smell of cheap aftershave.

Mum and Dad are going to kill me. Mum and Dad are going to kill me. Mum and Dad are going to kill me.

I pass a greasy coffee shop

I pass a greasy coffee shop and someone yells my name. I look into a window and Serena, her blonde hair falling across her tired eyes, is waving at me. She brings a coffee to her lips and beckons me inside. At the counter a heavy Lebanese man is reading a newspaper, looks up for a moment, then averts his eyes. The smell of burning fat and the mild odour of tobacco coats the air in the shop. I order a coffee, and pull a soft-drink from the fridge; my lips are dry, cracking. I run my tongue over them.

-Where's Maria? I ask. Serena says she doesn't give a fuck and offers me a cigarette. I take it and sit on a chair opposite. My body sags into the plastic, and I stare across at her. The drugs are still a poison in my system. I notice her eyes are red. I light the cigarette and try to think of something to say. But she begins the conversation.

-We had a fight. I don't answer and she continues.

-We had a fight and I asked to be dropped off here, told her I was going to wait for the first train and then go home. She cradles her coffee cup. Except the first train has gone and I'm still here.

-What did you argue about? I'm too strung out to talk to her. Too much has already happened tonight, I'm too tired. I don't want conversation, I want a joint, or a Valium. The Lebanese guy brings me my coffee and I hungrily gulp up the sour stinging fluid. Serena doesn't answer my question. Instead she asks me a question.

-What happened to the guy you picked up? I shrug my shoulders and look out the window. People are going to church, the Easybeats are on the radio. He left without me, I answer and I feel a tear is stinging in my pupil, bursting to come loose. I don't let it. Serena doesn't pursue it. She begins to answer my question.

-I was drunk, I guess. I asked her to sleep with me. She begins to laugh. And of course she said no and of course I got embarrassed and of course I got fucked off. She begins a quiet sob. I'm a dickhead, I'm a dickhead, she mutters and I look away again, out to the world beyond the coffee-shop window. Her story continues, and she begins to tell me about her love for the other woman, tells me that she has

been seeking a wog to love, someone who will understand
her, for a long, long time. Tells me she's tired of Aussie
dykes, dykes who can't converse, can't express emotion,
can't be affectionate. At twenty-one, she already sounds so
exhausted. Nearly twenty, I sound exhausted. I am exhausted.
The story she weaves comes in and out of my ears and I
listen to the sound of her voice, listen to bad songs from
the sixties on the radio.

-Do your parents know? She's asking me a question.

-Know what?

-That you are gay? Am I? I want to say. I want to tell her
that words such as faggot, wog, poofter, gay, Greek, Australian,
Croat are just excuses. Just stories, they mean shit. Words
don't stop the boredom. Instead I shake my head. No, I tell
her, they don't know. She laughs and takes my hand. Her
fingernails are long, thin, painted scarlet.

-We have to protect them, Ari, she tells me.

-What do you mean, protect. I don't understand her.

-Protect them, she is insistent. So that the neighbours
don't talk, so the relatives don't talk. She is loud now. You
are protecting them, Ari, you don't tell them about your life
because you know what that will do to them.

-Like I care. Her face freezes over, she draws back into
her seat. She wanted a connection between us and there
isn't one. She cares. I don't. I'm protecting myself. Mum and
Dad are adults. They can protect themselves.

-You don't give much away, do you, Ari? She takes her hand
away from mine. I move mine under the table and clasp at my
knees. The woman before me is drunk, angry. I'm afraid she's
going to make a scene. Instead she starts sobbing again. I
scratch my face, try to say something, nothing comes out. She's
drunk, I'm drug-fucked. None of this connection between us
is real, it is all hallucinations. I find some words. You're beautiful, I tell her, and she is. Her pale soft skin and her dark eyes.
She smiles at me and thanks me.

-I have to go, and she rises from her seat. Tell your friend

Maria I'm finished with Greek girls. I'm going to stick to my own kind.

–Where do you live? I ask her. Sunshine, she answers, I'm a dyke from the West. It's a long way away, isn't it? I ask. For me it's just another suburb in this city of suburbs.

–Sure is. She asks me where I live. I point to the view outside. Here, I live here.

–I hate the suburbs. Serena hands me a five-dollar bill and I decline. She pushes it firmly in my hand. I pocket it and wipe her hair from her eyes. Get out of Sunshine, I tell her.

–Got to. And you, Ari. She kisses me on the cheek. Where the fuck do you go? Somewhere, I answer, somewhere with no wogs, no faggots, no skips. She laughs and the tears coating her pupils vanish.

–I'll see you there, she tells me. I shrug. Maybe. Life's a trip, isn't it, Ari. They are her final words to me. She walks out the door and doesn't look back, walks up Swan Street towards the station. Back to the suburbs.

There is this urban myth

There is this urban myth I once heard. It may be true. That the places where the wealthy reside in my city were built in the East because it meant when driving home the rich would not get the sun in their eyes. The squinting and the sunstroke fall to the poor scum in the western suburbs.

There is another urban myth. It is about solidarity. The myth goes something like this; we may be poor, may be treated like scum, but we stick together, we are a community. The arrival of the ethnics put paid to that myth in Australia. In the working-class suburbs of the West where communal solidarity is meant to flourish, the skip sticks with the skip, the wog with the wog, the gook with the gook, and the abo with the abo. Solidarity, like love, is a crock of shit. The rich don't fear the unionised worker, they don't fear the militant. They fear the crim, the murderer, the basher. Crime doesn't pay but it is the only form of rebellion open to us. And to survive the thief must eschew solidarity.

Us, them. I am neither. I don't belong to the West. The West of chemical-vomit skies. This is an industrial city, a metropolis of manufacturing plants and workshops for blue-collar labour. The noise of the factory was the soundtrack to our childhood. All vanishing. The factories are being pulled down, the skies are emptying of smoke, and the flat, dry ground of this city is now home to thousands and thousands of petite boxes where people who used to be workers live.

Community. Don't comprehend that word. The mania of our culture is the desire to accumulate and accumulate, to become richer, to become classier, to become more secure, wealthier. It is impossible to feel camaraderie if the dominant wish is to get enough money, enough possessions to rise above the community you are in. To become richer and wealthier than the people around you is to spit in their faces. And the wogs, being peasants, do it best. Possession of land, of more and more land, is the means by which an uneducated, diasporic community enables itself to rise in the New World and kick their brothers and sisters in the face, in the gut, in the balls, in the cunt. Beyond all else the peasant requires land to feel secure. But unlike the accumulation of consumer products or of money, there is a limit to the availability of land. This is why wogs turn on each other. They have migrated to escape the chaos of history and they know, they know fundamentally, property is war.

The West at night, as you drive over the Westgate Bridge, is a shimmering valley of lights. In the day, under the harsh glare of the sun, the valley reveals itself as an industrial quilt of wharfs, factories, warehouses, silos and power plants. And the endless stretch of suburban housing estates. The West is a dumping ground; a sewer of refugees, the migrants, the poor, the insane, the unskilled and the uneducated. There is a point in my city, underneath the Swanston Street Bridge where you can sit by the Yarra River and contemplate the chasm that separates this town. Look down the river towards the East and there are green parks rolling down to the river, beautiful Victorian bridges sparkle against the blue sky. Face West and there is the smoke-scarred embankment leading towards the wharfs. The beauty and the beast. All cities, all cities depend on this chasm. All cities, from Melbourne to Karachi, New York to Istanbul, Paris to Nairobi, include sewers for the international human refuse that keeps being churned out through war, famine, unemployment, poverty. The insane migrant will pack some bags and leave the shithole they were born in for the promise of better pay and a better life somewhere else.

There is no America. There is no New World. There is no future available to the refo and the wog any more. Nowhere to run, like the song. They don't need factories any more, they have elegantly-sculptured machines powered by microchips. They don't need labour any more. Not now, now that they have the Internet. Nowhere to run, like the song. The sewers keep filling up, they are fucking overflowing and the refuse is choking up the atmosphere. From Singapore to Beijing, from Rio to Johannesburg.

There is a last, and very cherished, urban myth. That every new generation has it better than the one that came before it. Bullshit. I am surfing on the down-curve of capital. The generations after this are not going to build on the peasants' landholdings. There's no jobs, no work, no factories, no wage packet, no half-acre block. There is no more land. I am sliding towards the sewer, I'm not even struggling against the flow. I can smell the pungent aroma of shit, but I'm still breathing.

I watch Serena

I watch Serena walk slowly towards the station. A Vietnamese family walk past me, the thin husband holding the hand of a chattering, smiling young girl. The woman walks a little behind, looking into the shop windows. I smile at them and the man returns a hesitant smile back to me. The woman refuses to acknowledge me. They walk past me, up the hill, disappearing in the glare of the sunlight. I watch them, fascinated. A long time ago I was a chattering child, walking with my family along this strip of road, walking up the hill. I'm thinking that in a few years those parents are going to want to kill that chattering child, are going to worry themselves sick over the chattering child. I'm thinking, Christ, Mum and Dad are going to kill me.

My body is still pumped from the drugs. My head is hurting, a tiny pinprick of pain somewhere close to my forehead, a pain that pushes back onto my skull and affects my whole nervous system. My jaw is clenched. My cock feels heavy on my groin, bruised from the sex. I put one foot forward and begin a slow walk towards home. There is the sound of trams, cars, the familiar voices of shopowners, the familiar landscape in which I have spent all my life. I'm beginning to hate this city, hate its fucking familiarity. I want to go away, get out of here. I put on the headphones, press play and the music pushes my thoughts way back to some space in my head where I can't hear them. In the voluptuous thunder and rhythms of the Walkman I disappear and I am out of here.

I pass a couple of street kids

I pass a couple of street kids on my way up the hill. One's black, one's white, one's wog. They smell of solvents and petrol and are way out of it, eyes rolling to the back of their heads. I've never done glue; sniffed it once and it burnt my lungs. There is a generation coming after me that is fucking up faster than mine.

The wog kid looks like Johnny. This makes me sad. Is there something I have to apologise to Johnny for? I can't remember.

Johnny tells me all the time, move out kid. He tells me that I'm a faggot and that I'm a faggot for life. Johnny warns me to not go overboard on the chemicals. Watch them kid, he says, they'll dull the brain and they'll dull the soul.

Johnny has Toula. His dresses and skirts are also battle fatigues. He can't remain silent. Silence would kill Johnny.

The sun is very harsh and the hill seems neverending. One foot moves sluggishly after the other. I think of Johnny, think of him calling me gutless in one of his drunken rages. I fantasise that when I get home, I'll yell at Mum and Dad that I am leaving, that I've found a man and I'm going to move in with him. I can feel myself smiling in the open street, dreaming of a little house by the sea with George and me in it. But I smell solvents and the fantasy evaporates under the hot sun's glare. I'm so slow from the come-down that I couldn't say a word to my parents. I couldn't make a sound.

I'm nearly home and maybe it is not glue on the street kids I'm smelling. Maybe I'm smelling the residue of chemicals on my own skin. Johnny tries to tell me things all the time, prepare me for the way the real world works. But I move too sluggishly to care about making it to the real world. Johnny is right but he has Toula.

Drugs keep me quiet. And relatively content.

Fast forward

Fast forward. Fast forward past birth, early childhood, school. Pause. Pause at being in church and looking up at Christ in the *Panagia's* arms. A glance free of terror, or fear, free of adoration or love. Like looking at a schoolyard photo. Jesus could be any boy standing and smiling next to you. Off, pause.

Fast forward to an old man, a drunk putting his hands between my legs. I enjoy it. Some cousin's party, some uncle. Play. Not some uncle, it's my father's brother. He has a name. *Theo* Yianni. Rewind. Peeking through a half–open door. Watching my mother and father go for it, slamming hard into each other. Or rather my father slamming hard into my mother. Her arse high in the air. My hands on my dick. I'm shocked at how hairy her arse is.

Fast forward, past Jesus, past the uncle with his hands down my pants. Weddings, engagements, parties, all the cousins sitting around swapping dirty jokes and gossip. The clock on the classroom wall. Watching it, waiting for the day to be over. Pause. An old woman across the street laughs at me. Her neighbours, three old toothless Greek grandmas laughing at me. She points at my crotch. I look down, my zip undone, a piece of my penis hanging out. I scream at them. Fucking cunts, fucking cunts, fucking cunts. They keep laughing and mother comes out and bashes me hard against the side of my head. I'm dragged screaming into the house.

Fast forward. First joint, first party without the folks, first kiss, first jerk–off with a boy, first fail at school, first time getting drunk with Johnny.

Press play. Peter and me share a bong. I promise not to tell Alex in case she tells our parents. She's asleep in her room. I cough into the bong. Johnny is there and he laughs at me. Peter tells me he hates it at home, hates it. I don't have to say anything, he knows I know. We have Joy Division's *Closer* on the stereo. Pause. Johnny looks at Peter with what I thought then was adoration. Now I know it is a look of lust.

Fast forward past movies. Sneaking into *Caligula*. Bragging about it at school. Watching porn, buying records, then

buying CDs, first fuck with a girl. First time getting my arse
fucked. First snort of speed, first acid, first hit of speed, first
taste of smack. Pause. Motherfucker scary thought. Am I
having safe sex? Play. Instructions. Watching a nervous
young teacher demonstrate how to use a condom on a
carrot. Everyone laughing, me included, sitting on my burning
arse, wondering about the sperm gone up me, gone in me,
gone through me.

Fast forward through more instructions. This is how you
fuck, this is how you drink, this is how you take drugs, this
is how you treat a girl, this is how you recycle your garbage,
this is how you save the planet, this is how you can make a
difference. Pause. Play. We are the world. Play. Play that
funky music white boy. Fast forward. Failing school, signing
up for the dole, uncles, friends, aunts, neighbours telling you
about some shit job going in some shit store in some shit
street in some shit suburb. Play. Say no thanks. Dole office
sends you for an interview. Bald man, not looking at you,
looking out the window, asks what you want to be. I say I
don't know. Asks why you want to work in his store, in his
factory, in his office. I shrug my shoulders, don't say the
truth that I don't want to work in his fucking store, his
fucking factory, his fucking office. I say, don't know. Interview
lasts ten minutes. Go back to the dole office.

Fast forward. Past Peter leaving home, past Dad getting
drunk and chucking me out of home. Mum comes crying,
finds me at my aunt watching cheapo Greek video. Cradles
me and I'm embarrassed.

Fast forward. Parties, getting pissed, getting high, getting
stoned. Pause. Peter introduces me to Janet, to his housemate,
George. Fast fucking forward. More parties, getting drunk,
getting high, getting stoned. At some strange party, in some
strange bedroom, George sucks me, I suck him. We don't
connect. I ain't ever going to connect. Stop tape. Press
record.

There is no way out of this boring life unless you have

lots of money. Unless you are born with lots of money it takes a lifetime to make lots of money. Hard work bores me. I ain't no worker.

I'm ruled by my cock. I see someone I think is attractive and I want to be with them, taste them, put my cock in their face or up their arse or through their cunt. I can't imagine any of this ever changing. Marriage is out.

I'm not Australian, I'm not Greek, I'm not anything. I'm not a worker, I'm not a student, I'm not an artist, I'm not a junkie, I'm not a conversationalist, I'm not an Australian, not a wog, not anything. I'm not left wing, right wing, centre, left of centre, right of Genghis Khan. I don't vote, I don't demonstrate, I don't do charity.

What I am is a runner. Running away from a thousand and one things that people say you have to be or should want to be. They'll tell you God is dead but, man, they still want you to have a purpose. They'll point to a child and say there it is, that's purpose, that's meaning. That's bullshit. A child is a mass of cells and tissues and muscle that will grow up and will become Jack the Ripper or the president of the world. Maybe. More likely it will grow up and become a dole statistic. Worse, it will grow up and become an accountant. A child isn't a purpose, a child isn't meaning. A child is an accident that occurs when a piece of sperm bumps into an egg.

They'll point to someone working hard, point to my Mum or my Dad and say, look that's purpose. Work hard, dignity of labour. They'll point to two weak human beings who haven't got the guts to walk away into a lonely happiness, who year after year stick out jobs they hate and a marriage they can't breathe in for the sake of making some rich boss richer. They may have a house but the prick who owns the factories they work in has two houses, three houses, sixty fucking houses. There is no dignity without choice and there is no choice. I didn't choose to be a runner.

I like music, I like film. I'm going to have sex, listen to

music and watch film for the rest of my life. I am here, living my life. I'm not going to fall in love, I'm not going to change a thing, no one will remember me when I'm dead. My epitaph; he slept, he ate, he fucked, he pissed, he shat. He ran to escape history. That's his story.

Press stop. Tape is terminated.

Alex is drinking a coffee

Alex is drinking a coffee and flicking through a magazine when I get home. I sit down on the couch next to her and take a sip from her cup. She makes room for me and I take one of her cigarettes. Inner City's *Paradise* is on the stereo. Where's Mum and Dad? I ask. Gone to church. Yes, I shout with glee. By the time they are back I'll be asleep in bed. I've saved myself a lecture. I go into the kitchen and grab an orange juice. You still speeding? Alex questions me.

–Don't know. I sit down next to her and ask her questions about how her night was.

–Like shit. She throws me a dirty look. Charlie and I fought all night long. He thinks you hate him. I take a sip from my coffee. He's a jerk, I tell her.

–He thinks you were rude to him last night. I don't answer. My sister can hitch herself up to some uptight Muslim bastard who will make her life misery, but that isn't my concern. I'm not changing for Charlie. She pauses for a moment. His mum liked you, she thought you were a nice boy. I smile. I am, I say. Alex continues speaking, softly. I watch her as the words come out, her little girl face is marked with spots, her hair hangs limp. She hasn't slept yet. We fucked last night, she tells me.

–Bad move, I tell her. She nods. He thinks I'm not a virgin. You're not, I reply. She starts laughing. I know, but he doesn't. I told him I've used a vibrator. I look at her in amazement. You didn't? I ask her, and she continues laughing. Stops,

and with a smirk on her face says, I did tell him, I said it
was one of yours. For a moment I look at my sister and she
looks very young, and very frail, a small hurt animal floating
on the couch, and then I look at her grinning at me and I
start laughing with her. What did he say?

–He said it was disgusting but I think it excited him. He'll
be after your arse next. I finish the cigarette and go up to
the stereo. I work the CD select so I can hear *Big Fun*. The
song comes on and I sway to it, not looking at my sister. I
turn around. Stay away from wog boys, kiddo, I tell her,
they'll fuck you up.

Hey Ari, what am I going to do? I love the bastard. She
moves off the couch and grabs my hand.

–Alex, I say to her, I'm tired. Can we talk about this later?
She lets go of my hand, gives me a weird look and wipes a
tear from her eyes. Like you care, she whispers to me. Then
she begins shouting. I hate fucking Arabs she screams. I
move towards my bedroom. She's still screaming. I hate
fucking wogs. Fucking Greeks and Italians. I hate fucking
Australians and the fucking English. The fucking Chinese
and the fucking Vietnamese. Fucking Africans, fucking
Indians, fucking Aborigines. I hate them all she screams
down the corridor. She slams the door to her bedroom.

My head is spinning. I'm still drug-fucked. Out of it. Stoned.
High. Ripped. Pissed. Tripping. Loaded. I want to go to Alex
and tell her that I may be in love. That I think I'm going to
be a faggot for the rest of my life. That I'm exhausted and
want her to hold me. My head begins to spin more and I
wonder if Alex has any drugs to smoke.

I get into bed and lie there for five minutes, ten minutes,
half-an-hour looking at the ceiling. It's not like I'm thinking.
No thought goes through my head. I look at the walls and
the ceiling. My hands are playing with my balls. I'm not even
thinking about sex, not thinking about anyone or anything.
I'm just looking at the ceiling.